ANGEL'S TEARS

Born in the same year that the Titanic sank, seventeen-year-old Cassandra Grant has the world at her feet. But tragedy strikes her family and Cassie has to grow up fast. She falls in love with Dr Michael Ryan — but then discovers he is about to be engaged to be married. Cassie leaves town to begin training as a midwife and tries to forget Michael, but tragedy strikes again and she has to return home where there are more surprises in store . . .

TERESA ASHBY

ANGEL'S TEARS

Complete and Unabridged

LINFORD
Leicester

First published in Great Britain in 1989

First Linford Edition
published 2013

A catalogue record for this book is available
from the British Library.

ISBN 978–1–4448–1718–8

Published by
F. A. Thorpe (Publishing)
Anstey, Leicestershire

Set by Words & Graphics Ltd.
Anstey, Leicestershire
Printed and bound in Great Britain by
T. J. International Ltd., Padstow, Cornwall

This book is printed on acid-free paper

1

It had been a wonderful summer, but then, aren't all summers wonderful when you're young? Cassandra Grant, born in the same year that the Titanic went down, smiled to herself just with the sheer joy of being alive!

The boat train was waiting just in front of her, empty of passengers, but clean and scrubbed, the pride of the line and all those who worked on her. The wheeltapper appeared at the far end of the platform and began his journey along the length of the train, tapping each wheel as he went.

Tap-tap, tap-tap. He hesitated by one of the wheels, tapped again, then smiled to himself and moved on.

''Morning, Mr Atkins,' Cassie called out.

''Morning to you, Miss Cassie.' He stopped what he was doing and raised his hat, then quickly recommenced his wheeltapping.

Cassie, who was sitting upon the low stone wall surrounding the stationmaster's prized rose beds, plucked absent-mindedly at one of the remaining blooms on a bush, yelping involuntarily when a thorn pierced her finger.

'You'll get a cold in your old age, sitting there,' Henry, a station porter, commented. He was a good-looking lad, at eighteen, a year older than Cassie. His blue eyes twinkled whenever he spoke to her and Cassie wondered why, when he could have his choice of the local girls, he seemed so taken with her.

'Oh, Henry.' She gasped, pretending to be horrified. 'What have you spilled on your jacket?'

She pointed her finger at his chest and Henry turned a satisfactory shade of pink.

'Spilled? Me? Nothin'!'

Panic stricken, he pressed his chin against his chest, trying in vain to see the imaginary stain. The stationmaster always insisted that his staff were as neatly turned out as his locomotives and carried out a thorough uniform check shortly before the ship arrived.

'Have you got a hanky, Cass?' he said urgently, still trying to see what wasn't there.

Cassie was having difficulty hiding her laughter. Her dark eyes sparkled with tears of mirth and she clamped her teeth so hard together that it made her jaws ache.

Her hair, a flowing mane of dark, rebellious curls formed a halo around her face. Her skin, although very pale, had a healthy glow and she was, she was often told, the very image of her late mother.

'Where is it?' Henry was still twisting and turning and Cassie poked her finger at his chest.

'There,' she said, bringing her finger up quickly and catching him under the chin. 'Got you!'

'Why you . . . ' Henry's panic turned

to rage, then blessed relief.

Cassie jumped down from the wall, catching her petticoat on the rough stone and tearing a long ragged strip from the hem, but she was laughing too much to notice as Henry chased her along the platform.

'Just you wait!' he called, puffing and panting as he tried in vain to catch her. Cassie was swift on her feet and dodged around the seats and lamp posts with ease.

Henry kept on chasing her until there was nowhere left to hide — then Cassie saw him. A young man standing just along the platform. He was well-dressed, but apart from that, she was in too much of a hurry to notice much else as she ran around him.

Henry cornered her and without thinking, she clasped the man around the waist as she dodged from side to side, the laughter tearing at her throat. Somehow, she had caught her hand in his jacket pocket and as she ran around him the pocket tore.

'Hey!' the man cried. 'Do you mind?'

Cassie was mortified at what she'd done and stared at the man in absolute terror. He looked angry enough to strike her and his deep, blue eyes blazed.

At that moment, the ship blew and everything stopped.

'The boat,' Henry gasped, straightening his clothes.

'My dad!' Cassie cried jubilantly, the chase forgotten as she stood up on her toes for the first glimpse of the spiral of black smoke which signalled the arrival of the ship, carrying her much-loved father.

The station staff poured on to the platform, getting into line ready for the stationmaster's inspection and Cassie took off for the quay, the ragged tail of her petticoat trailing along behind her.

She reached the quayside in time to see the ship coming around the point and began to wave her arms furiously. The decks were adorned with bunting and passengers lined the rails. Some of them returned her waves.

She scanned the decks for some sight of her father, but he was nowhere to be seen and her excitement abated somewhat. It would be a while before the ship was alongside and she turned her gaze out to the sea which was as blue as could be beneath the clear October sky. The blue of the sky put her in mind of the eyes of the man on the station and she shivered despite herself.

Gulls wheeled and dived above the water, skimmed the surface then soared towards the sun, their wings flashing like silver and Cassie shivered again, this time in delight. She wondered what her father had brought home for her this trip. Last time it had been the leather, lace-up boots she now wore, hand made by the same Dutch cobbler who, a couple of months before, had sent her a pair of real wooden clogs.

Her warm jacket had come from Norway, her dress from France and her soft, warm gloves from Sweden and Cassie had long ago decided that she was truly Continental! It was certainly true that she was better dressed than most of her peers.

She took a deep breath. There was still a slight smell of fish in the air, even though the fishermen had landed their catch hours ago and it had all been auctioned off at the quayside before being taken away to Billingsgate.

At the west end of the quay, men worked non-stop at the shipbuilding yard, creating magnificent and graceful vessels that would one day sail the oceans of the world. Cassie's eyes shone when she thought of all those far away exotic lands that her father had told her about.

He had sailed to them all and always brought back with him gifts and tales to bring her endless delight.

Since his marriage to Ivy and the birth of their two sons, Jack and David, Cassie's father had taken up a position on the continental runs, which was fine by Cassie because it meant that she saw even more of him.

To the east, the ship had been tied up and the shore gang were hurrying to push the big gangway into position, ready for the eager feet of the passengers. A veritable army of porters and lads from the town waited, ready to fetch and carry for the passengers and earn themselves a few farthings.

Cassie took her time walking to the ship. The crew were always last to come off and her father, being the Captain, liked to make sure everything was in order before leaving the vessel in the hands of the watch.

Down below her, a family of swans bobbed on the muddy waters that lapped against the quay. She wished she'd had the boys with her. Jack was five, David seven. They'd have liked to see the big white birds with their brown, fluffy young. Or maybe they wouldn't, she smiled wryly.

They were not like her, she reminded herself. In fact, they were as different from her as could be, something she was never able to forget.

Watching the passengers disembark with their wonderful array of trunks and packages, Cassie drifted off into a world of her own, only emerging when the quayside was deserted. In the distance, she heard a shrill whistle, then the chug of the train as it pulled away from the platform, full to bursting with the passengers off the boat.

The time! Swinging round, she saw the church clock. It was half past one! She should have been home for lunch an hour ago. Ivy would be fit to be tied, but if Cassie could walk in on her father's arm, he'd stand between the two of them like a rock.

Then she saw him. He came out on deck with his hat in his hand, then he pulled it on over his sandy hair, carefully straightening it so that it sat just-so before he ran down the gangway. Cassie dashed to meet him, running into his arms as though he'd been away for weeks instead of just days.

'Hello, Angel.' He smiled. 'Have you

been waiting long?'

'Ages,' she said, falling into step beside him, hanging onto his arm. 'Was it a good trip?'

'It was pleasant enough,' he said and the faraway look in his eyes told Cassie that a part of him still longed to sail to those distant, exotic countries.

'What did you see?'

'The sea.' He laughed and ruffled her untidy hair. 'And I haven't brought you anything back this time, Angel. I was a bit off colour when we got to the other side and I didn't go ashore.'

'Are you all right now?' Cassie asked anxiously.

'Perfectly,' he replied. 'Don't look so worried. It was just a gippy tummy, that's all.'

Even so, there were lines of strain etched around his eyes and he looked paler than usual. The ruddy glow normally in his cheeks wasn't there and no matter what he said, Cassie was worried.

Their house, in a quiet tree-lined avenue just fifteen minutes' walk from the quay, had been built for James Grant and his bride, Prudence Scott who had been Cassie's beautiful mother.

Although Prudence had died before Cassie was of an age to remember her, Cassie fancied that the house still retained the spirit of her mother. Or perhaps it was the encompassing spirit of her grandmother who had raised her until she, too, died.

It was a strange feeling, knowing that this tall, handsome man was her only family. His parents were both dead and that left just the two of them. But there was Ivy. Ivy was a nice enough woman, but not overly fond of Cassie, or so it seemed to the younger girl.

'I don't have my key, Angel,' James Grant said.

'I'll knock then,' Cassie said and did so.

Through the stained glass panels of

the upper door, she could see a black shape coming down the hall in answer to their knock. It was Mary, the maid and when she opened the door, she looked quite shocked.

'You're late,' she hissed at Cassie, casting anxious glances at the Captain.

'That's all right, Mary,' James said easily. 'Cassie can eat her lunch with me.'

'But . . . ' Mary's face went red. 'But . . . '

'It is most certainly not all right.' Ivy Grant swept into the hall. She was small, dark-haired and green-eyed and Cassie had never seen her look so cross.

'That's the third time this week she hasn't come home for her lunch — and she has to do it today of all days.'

'What's special about today?' James asked.

'You're as bad as she is! I told you a dozen times, James, that I would be entertaining Doctor Morgan and his godson! How do you think it looked to have one empty place at the table?'

Cassie's hand flew to her mouth and her eyes widened.

'I'm sorry,' she cried. 'I completely forgot.'

'Cassie, I despair of you,' Ivy said, her face softening. 'You're not a child any longer. You're a young woman and soon you'll be away at college.'

'Are they still here?' James asked.

'In the drawing room,' Ivy said. 'I've apologised, but how must it look, James?'

Ivy looked close to despair. She was constantly worrying about what other people thought of her.

'Come along, let's go and meet them . . . ' He stepped towards the drawing room and Ivy threw up her hands in horror when she saw the state Cassie was in.

'She looks like a ragamuffin! You've torn your petticoat, Cassie, and look at your hair! And she smells of fish, James.'

But James could see nothing wrong with his daughter and led her forcefully into the drawing room.

Doctor Morgan and his godson stood at once. Cassie knew the doctor well. He was her godfather, too, and very fond of her. She knew that his godson, at present training to be a doctor himself, was presently staying with Doctor Morgan for a while.

'Hello, Uncle Philip.' Cassie rushed over and kissed the doctor on the cheek. 'I'm sorry I missed lunch, but I was waiting for Dad and I lost all track of time.'

Philip Morgan held her at arm's length and smiled adoringly at her. He never failed to make her feel extra special.

'Ah, what it is to be young,' he chuckled. 'Now, Cassie, I want you to meet Michael, who, like you, is my godchild. I think you may have met him before, when you were both small, but . . .'

Cassie turned to look at the stranger and her stomach seemed to turn over inside her. Yes, she vaguely recalled a plump little boy who had come to

14

spend the summer with Uncle Philip years and years ago . . . but this!

He was tall. Taller even than her father, with dark hair and dark, sapphire blue eyes. She stared at him, sure she knew those so-blue eyes. He wore expensive clothes and as soon as she saw the torn pocket of his jacket, she knew exactly why he had seemed so familiar.

'Hello, James.' The doctor was speaking to Cassie's father now. 'This is my godson, Michael Ryan.'

Michael Ryan was glaring at Cassie so that she trembled in her hand-made boots. For once in her life, she wished she had behaved like a young lady today. Even her easy going father would be angry if he knew what she'd done.

She lifted her chin defiantly as Michael held out his hand and put her own hand inside. He took it in a grip so firm that she thought the bones in her hand would break.

'Will you be staying here long?' she said.

15

'I hope to settle here once I've qualified,' he said, fixing her with those hypnotic eyes. 'If it suits.'

'I don't see why it shouldn't suit you,' she said impertinently. 'This is a perfectly nice town.'

'It depends what you're used to,' he answered and Cassie's blood began to boil as it always did if anyone tried to criticise her home.

'You've torn your pocket,' she said, her eyes sparkling with mischief, daring him to tell on her.

'I didn't tear it,' he said coolly. 'I was reacquainting myself with the town and by a stroke of misfortune, found myself on the railway station. A foolish little girl was playing around with one of the young porters. She was running around like a wild animal, in fact, she almost knocked me down.'

Cassie felt her cheeks burn. He hadn't told on her, but he had made her feel stupid and childish, just when she wanted to appear adult.

'I can't understand the parents,

letting them run wild like that,' Ivy commented.

'The parents probably don't know,' Michael said.

'I'll mend it for you, if you like,' Cassie said in a belated effort to make amends.

'That's very kind of you.' He slipped the jacket off his wide shoulders and handed it to her and for the first time she saw those lovely eyes smile.

Ivy and James stared at Cassie as she hurried off in search of the sewing basket. Usually she went to great pains to avoid needlework of any kind. Ivy smiled. Perhaps she was rather taken by the handsome, young man.

In a way, she hoped so. It would be nice if Cassie were off her hands and she had James all to herself without the image of his late wife flitting around like a spectre, always ready to come between them.

Cassie sat right down and mended the jacket, her tongue poking out of the side of her mouth as she sewed. Once or twice, she looked up and caught Michael Ryan looking at her. Then he'd wink and her face would flood with colour and she'd stare once again at her needle and thread.

'It's perfect, Cass,' he said when she'd finished. 'Thank you very much.'

'My pleasure.' She smiled.

'Now we should go,' Philip Morgan said, getting reluctantly to his feet. 'We have a great deal to attend to this afternoon.'

'I expect we'll meet again,' Michael said softly so only Cassie could hear.

'I hope so.' She grinned.

2

After a few hours at home, her father's ship was ready to sail again and James set off at a brisk walk towards the quay. Cassie had been told to stay at home and she sat by the window, watching until her father had disappeared from sight.

'What did you think of Michael Ryan, Cassie?' Ivy asked, looking up from her knitting. 'He seemed very nice to me.'

'I think he's nice,' Cassie said.

'Just nice, Cassie?' Ivy smiled.

'I'm bored,' Cassie said, changing the subject and resting her chin on her hands.

'You could always go and read to the boys,' Ivy suggested. 'It will be good practice for when you're a teacher and besides, they're bored, too.'

'You should let them out to play

then,' Cassie retorted. 'All the other boys play on the mud, they feel left out.'

Ivy's face reddened.

'They're not like the other boys, Cassie.'

'Yes they are,' she argued. 'I was always allowed to play out when I was little.'

'But you were . . . ' Ivy broke off and bit her lip.

Cassie got up and walked wordlessly from the room. She was different. Yes, she knew. Her mother had been beautiful, but from a humble family who had lived in rented rooms just off the docks.

She had grown up with the feeling that she didn't really belong anywhere, so she carved a path of her own right down the middle.

* * *

The next time her father's ship was due in, Ivy made Cassie stay in until after lunch. She was itching to get down to

20

the quay and ate her food with a speed that made Ivy tut and the boys giggle.

Even in their dining room, so far from the quay, Cassie heard the ship blow and the look of panic that came into her eyes made Ivy laugh and relent.

'All right,' she said, a twinkle in her eye. 'Run along.'

Run she did, all the way down to the quay, through the narrow, ancient streets of the town, past the many pubs and the Trinity yard, until by the time she got there, she was out of breath and red in the face.

The ship was alongside, passengers were coming off. Less in numbers now the summer had gone. Her father was up on deck, staring out seemingly at nothing.

He was a dreamer. Cassie wondered what he was dreaming about now.

She waited patiently at the bottom of the gangway until he came down. Not at a trot like he usually did, but slowly. His face was drawn and seemed to have grown thinner since she last saw him.

21

Instead of holding out his arms to her as he usually did, he walked right past, not even acknowledging her presence. She stared after him a moment, looking at his wide back, expecting him at any moment to spin round and laugh, but he didn't.

He started to walk faster away from her, his legs moving in long, purposeful strides.

'Daddy!' She gave chase. Her legs ached from running down here and she had to struggle to keep up with him.

'Daddy!' she called again, her voice cracking.

Like a man in a trance, he stopped dead and turned slowly around. She stopped behind him, gasping for breath, her chest aching with a pain that seemed to have its roots deep inside.

She looked up at him, so tall and handsome in his uniform, but like a stranger with his arctic cold eyes and grim, set mouth.

'What's happened?' she asked, her voice small.

The big, carefree man now looked like someone with the problems of the whole world on his shoulders. The hardness in his eyes vanished and despair took its place. His whole face seemed to crumble.

'Are you ill?'

'The news came over the ship's wireless,' he said, a tear falling from his eye and hurrying down his cheek.

Cassie didn't know whether to be embarrassed or sorry. She'd never seen a man cry before and right out here in the street ... she looked around nervously, but the street was empty.

'What news?' Cassie had little time for news. It was boring and depressing and if it didn't touch her life, she saw no reason to either bore or depress herself. She was young and enjoying her youth, but somewhere deep inside, there was a grown up trying to emerge and take control.

'I have to get a newspaper,' he said, turning around. Cassie followed at a trot, racking her brains, trying to think what had happened over the past few days.

The big news had been the disaster at the New York Stock Exchange on Wall Street. Repercussions were already being felt here, but surely that wouldn't cause her father such grief.

He stopped abruptly a few yards from the news stand and rubbed his big hands across his face. He sighed deeply.

'What am I doing?' He turned to look at Cassie.

She shook her head.

'I'm sorry, Angel,' he said. 'Come with me. I have to talk to you . . . to explain.'

They walked in silence to the other side of town where wide greenswards stretched all the way down to the beach. It was a favourite place for women to push their babies, for children to play and for men to take their sweethearts, but now it was deserted.

There was an old wooden bench on the promenade and James Grant told

Cassie to sit down, then he took off his hat, hesitated a moment and sat down beside her.

They sat in silence for a few minutes, staring out to the sea. It was sparkling with dots of sunlight that leapt and danced across the wavelets while closer to them, it washed back and forth across the shingle making a gentle shushing sound.

'Tell me,' she said.

He ran his tongue over his lips nervously and turned his hat round and round in his hands.

'The fact is, Angel, I've lost just about everything. I put all my money in shares and . . .'

'But Ivy told you not to!' Cassie burst out.

'I did it anyway.' He smiled thinly. 'I believe I may have ruined us.'

The lines on his forehead seemed to fade then, as though by saying it out loud, he had somehow relieved some of the burden.

'That's not so bad,' Cassie said

cheerfully, ever the optimist. 'We have the house and you still have a job.'

'Oh, Angel.' He laughed and put his arm around her shoulders. 'Where would I be without you? Ivy will shout and be cross and tearful, but you . . . '

Cassie frowned. Of course Ivy would be cross and tearful. She had two little boys to think of. It was easy for Cassie to be cheerful as she had none of the responsibilities.

'Poor Ivy,' she said.

James stared at her, puzzled, and for Cassie, it was like seeing him for the first time. Ivy was always saying he was irresponsible and she was right. He did nothing to discourage Cassie's defiance, in fact, the conflict always bubbling beneath the surface between his daughter and his wife, seemed to amuse him.

Could this man she idolised really be so shallow? No, she decided, not shallow, never shallow. He was just Dad, a dreamer, that's the way he was. He believed fervently in the power of dreams, so much so that he sometimes seemed to have difficulty separating the dream from the reality.

'Don't look at me like that, Angel,' he pleaded.

She forced herself to smile, but wondered if the future held the same fate for her. She was very like him, but she didn't want to remain a child forever.

Just as quickly as he'd cheered up, his face crumpled and he began to cry. Cassie folded her thin arms around him and held him tight, stroking his hair as though he were a child.

It was a funny thing about sailors. They were an emotional breed, easy to laugh, easy to cry. Grandma said it was because they lived so close to nature, often finding themselves at the mercy of the elements. Some of them were very religious, some were poets, a few were dreamers.

Cassie got to her feet and held out her hand.

'Let's go home,' she said. 'Ivy will be worried.'

27

'I can't face her, Angel,' he said.

'Yes you can and you must.'

He smiled at her through his tears, a smile full of warmth and tenderness.

'You're so like your mother,' he said softly. 'It sometimes hurts me just to look at you.'

And Cassie knew that despite his years of marriage to Ivy, he was still in love with Prudence and always would be.

She knew too that the time had come to start growing up. He'd kept her a child too long, but it was time she made some decisions of her own.

'Am I like her?' she said. 'I know I look like her, but . . . '

'Oh, you're very like her.' He smiled sadly. 'My Pru was headstrong and wilful, sometimes a little selfish, always warm.'

Cassie's eyebrows went up. Was she headstrong and wilful? She knew she was sometimes selfish and it was an aspect of her nature she was trying very hard to alter.

'Perhaps I'm to blame, I've always spoiled you.'

Spoiled? Cassie began to seriously wonder whether she was a very nice person at all.

* * *

The house had never looked so welcoming. As always, James had no key and Cassie had to knock and as usual, it was Mary who hurried to answer.

'I wondered where you'd got to.' Ivy came out of the drawing room. She looked strained and Cassie realised that she'd been gone a long time to meet her father.

'I'm sorry,' James said. 'My fault.'

Cassie was astounded at how controlled he sounded now, a far cry from the man who had wept in her arms on the seafront.

Apart from a slight redness around his eyes, there was no indication of his breakdown and everything seemed almost normal.

'There's something wrong,' Ivy said, her eyes darting from Cassie to James. 'My God . . . you did it, didn't you?' she gasped.

James hung his head and Cassie fidgetted uncomfortably. Mary slipped away to the kitchen, leaving them to it.

'I warned you!' Ivy's voice rose. 'You wouldn't listen to me though, would you? No, you knew better! A man like you can't afford to dabble in things you know nothing about! How much have you lost?'

'Go up to your room, Angel,' he said, then, taking Ivy by the arm, led her into the drawing room and shut the door firmly between them.

Cassie did not go to her room. She waited where she was for a moment, then ran to the door and listened.

'Don't touch me!' Ivy's voice was loud, upset. 'How could you do this, James? How could you?'

'If things had gone well, then we'd have been rich one day, I mean really rich, Ivy.'

30

'I never wanted to be rich, you fool.' She was crying now. 'I was happy as we were . . . or as happy as I could ever hope to be.'

'What's that supposed to mean?'

'You know what I'm talking about, James. It's her, isn't it? Prudence. You see, even if I mention her name, you get that look on your face. I see it in your eyes every time you look at Cassie, hear it in your voice when you speak to her.'

'Don't, Ivy . . . '

'You're weak, you always have been, but I never thought you would bring us to this. How bad is it? Do you know yet?'

Poor Ivy, Cassie thought again. All this time she felt sure her stepmother resented her, even hated her at times, now she knew why.

Her father's voice murmured so low that she couldn't make out the words, but Ivy's voice remained strong and clear.

'We'll manage somehow,' she said. 'Even if it means that Cassie has to go out to work.'

'No!'

Cassie, flinched. She had never heard him sound so angry before.

'Why not? She's old enough to work and they pay well at the factory.'

'I promised her mother that she'd never have to work in the factory,' he said. 'It's a promise I intend to keep.'

'Even if it means the rest of us starve?'

'Don't be ridiculous, it won't come to that.'

'Do you honestly believe that that girl is ever going to settle down at college? You're always saying that she's got a lot of her mother in her! And now I have to see my life in ruins because of some promise you made years ago! Look at the money you spend on her! Always bringing her gifts home . . . when did you last bring anything home for me, James?'

Someone knocked on the door and Cassie jumped, not knowing which way to turn. The row continued in the drawing room. Mary did not emerge from the kitchen, so she hurried to answer the door herself.

'Miss Grant.' Michael Ryan grinned at her.

'Have you brought me something else to mend?' she demanded, flinching as she heard the raised voices coming from the drawing room. She had meant her remark to be taken as a joke, but even to her own ears, her voice sounded harsh.

'No, I . . . ' he broke off when Ivy's voice rose to a near scream. 'I can see I've come at a bad time,' he went on, clearly uncomfortable. 'Perhaps I should . . . '

'What did you want?' Cassie sighed. 'Can I help?'

'Perhaps.' He smiled. 'It was really your parents I came to see.'

'I am capable of taking a message,' she said. 'I've finished with chasing around on railway stations.'

'I'm glad to hear it.' He grinned.

She looked up at him. He really was quite nice looking when he wasn't angry. His face was rather angular, his features large, but not obtrusive and when he smiled, there were dimples in his cheeks.

She sighed again. 'Won't you come in?'

He stepped into the hall and wiped his feet on the mat.

'I'll . . . em . . . ' She stepped towards the drawing room, but it was her father who was shouting now and she felt confused. Should she interrupt them? Should she even have invited anyone into the house when they were having such an argument?

Ivy would never forgive her. Ivy who set so much store by appearances.

'I can't stay.' Michael was heading back towards the door. 'I have some patients to see at the infirmary.'

Cassie opened the door for him. She felt embarrassed. There was a crash in the drawing room and she stepped outside quickly and closed the door, shutting herself outside with Michael.

Violent rows didn't happen very often,

but when they got to the throwing-things-around stage, she wanted to be well away from it.

She looked up at Michael and laughed nervously, trying to behave as though nothing was amiss.

'I'll walk with you to the gate,' she said and set off down the path with him following.

Down by the gate, the argument raging inside the house was out of earshot — or over, Cassie wasn't sure which.

'Are you sure I can't help?' she said.

'Uncle Philip asked me to call by to invite your parents — and you — to the house for dinner next week. Tuesday if that's convenient.'

'I'm sure it will be.' She smiled. 'Are you sure the invitation includes me?'

'Positive.' Michael grinned. 'I especially asked Uncle Philip to include you.'

'I'll tell my stepmother to telephone you,' Cassie said, extremely flattered that he wanted to see her again after the terrible first impression she must have given.

'Thanks. I'll look forward to seeing you next week.'

Cassie stood at the gate for a long time after he'd driven away, deep in thought, still wondering why Michael Ryan wanted to see her again when she had behaved so badly before.

She concluded in the end that she amused him, what other possible reason could there be.

The house was silent as she re-entered through the side door which was never locked and she bumped into Mary in the hall, hurrying through with a brush and dustpan. She looked hot and flustered.

'Much?' Cassie whispered, looking uneasily at the study door.

'Two glasses and a dish.' Mary sniffed.

Upstairs, muffled through a door, Ivy's sobs could be heard. Cassie hesitated for a moment, then her father burst out of his study and marched towards the door.

'Where are you going?' she cried.

'Out,' he snapped, then he was gone, slamming the door behind him. Mary pulled a face, then hurried into the drawing room to clear up the mess and Cassie ran upstairs.

'What do you want?' Ivy looked up. Her face was scarlet and streaked with tears.

'Are you all right?'

'No, I'm not all right. Do I look all right?'

'I'm sorry. Is there anything I can get you?'

Ivy sat up and stared at Cassie, a steady stream of tears still pouring down her face.

'He's gone to get drunk,' she said.

'That's no answer,' Cassie said and Ivy looked surprised.

'I thought you were on his side,' she said.

'I'm not on anyone's side,' Cassie said. 'Would you like a cup of tea?'

'You're full of surprises today, Cass.'

Ivy said, dabbing at her tears with a lace handkerchief. 'Yes, I'd love some tea.'

★   ★   ★

It was dark and Cassie and her brothers were in bed when James finally came home. The gate crashed back and he stumbled up the path and fell against the front door. This time he had his key with him, but he couldn't get it in the lock.

Cassie lay in bed listening to the scrape of metal against metal. Ivy was waiting downstairs and she wondered if there'd be another row.

The front door opened and there was the murmur of voices. He was home. Thank goodness.

Outside, a storm was brewing. The wind was beginning to lick around the chimney pots and rustle the dry leaves in the trees.

Cassie didn't feel quite well.

She didn't think it was the events of the day, for she normally took most

38

things in her stride. She'd recently had a cold, but that had gone.

Relaxed now her father was home safe and suddenly very tired, Cassie drifted off to sleep.

It was much later that she awoke with a start. The wind was pounding against the house, rain clattered against the window panes, but above and beyond all that, another sound penetrated her sleep.

'Cassie!' It was Ivy, screaming. 'Cassie, wake up . . . for goodness sake, Cassie, come quickly.'

3

It took a moment or two for the sound to sink in. Downstairs, the shutters on the windows had come loose and were banging against the walls of the house. Outside her bedroom, the branches of the sycamore tree scratched at the window and all the time there was the relentless hiss of the rain as it battered the roof.

'Cassie!' Ivy again, screaming.

Cassie jumped from her bed and ran towards the door just as a jagged Z of lightning raked across the sky and flickered white light through her room. It was followed closely by a deafening rumble of thunder which shook the whole house.

The door burst open before she could reach it and Ivy stood there in her nightdress, her dark hair hanging loose around her shoulders, her black eyes almost wild, flickering in the light from the lamp clasped in her hand.

'Cassie . . . you have to go for the doctor. The telephone's dead and Mary refuses to go outside . . . No!' She slapped Cassie's hand away as she reached for the light switch. 'Not in this storm! Do you want to kill us all?'

Ivy's attitude had always bewildered Cassie. She had an irrational fear of electricity and in a storm such as this, would often run about the house covering all the mirrors with blankets.

Cassie yawned. It must be David or Jack, sick again. David probably, he was a bit of a sickly child, always ailing with one thing or another. It was because Ivy coddled them so.

'Hurry, oh, please, hurry,' Ivy urged.

Cassie, once she was dressed, realised that she was shaking uncontrollably. It was fear brought on by the storm and the sudden realisation that if a doctor was required in the middle of the night, it had to be something serious.

She loved both her little half-brothers

dearly, they had much of their father in them, despite inheriting their mother's dark colouring.

She laced up her boots without care, then ran downstairs where Mary was waiting, holding her coat.

'You mind how you go,' Mary said sternly. 'Put your hat on . . . '

Mary was twenty-eight, going on fifty! Her brown hair was already liberally flecked with grey and it seemed to Cassie that she must have been born middle-aged, never young.

'No time,' Cassie called back as she opened the door. The wind blasted in, forcing entry like a violent intruder, bringing with it a swirl of leaves and twigs that it had torn from the trees outside.

'Shut the door behind me,' she shouted to make herself heard above the wind and when Mary closed the door, she felt a sudden pang of fear.

She was outside, at the mercy of the storm and alone.

Thunder rumbled and crashed overhead, the wind roared through the trees and as she began to run from the garden, a slate crashed down from the roof, landing beside her on the path and shattering. She felt a sudden sharp pain in her leg, but ignored it.

Her dash through the empty streets was a nightmare. The doctor didn't live very far away, just a ten minute walk on a normal day, but Cassie was running against the wind, with rain stinging her eyes and her limbs aching with the effort.

Her chest hurt so much she could hardly breathe and her heart, thundering behind her ribs, didn't help the discomfort.

The wind plucked at her hair, tore it from the loose braids which she wore to sleep and tossed it around her head.

The doctor lived in a rather grand house on the seafront. It had been in his family for years. They had once been very wealthy and had at one time owned the clothing factory which provided so much work for the women in the town. The doctor still had a great deal of influence in the running of the factory even though his financial interests had ended a long time ago.

Cassie's boots, carelessly laced, tripped her so that she fell, sprawling on the pavement. Pain spiralled through her head and the cold seeped through her clothes, chilling her to the core.

It was an effort to pick herself up, but she managed it and began to run towards the house which was now in sight, a big, rugged building standing out even in the darkness against the emptiness of the sea beyond.

She leaned against the door and rang the bell, then desperation made her hammer with her fists. Lights came on inside, voices could be heard beyond the heavy door and she almost fainted with relief when the door opened and she was able to stumble inside.

'Good gracious!' Doctor Morgan was a small man with thinning grey hair and a neat moustache. Michael was there in the background, and so was Mrs Percival, the doctor's housekeeper.

The doctor put his arms around Cassie and led her inside to a chair.

'You're soaked through,' he said, trying to brush away the tangle of her hair from her face.

'Who is she, Uncle?' Michael asked. 'Do you know her?'

'I'm not sure ... but ... good gracious, I'd know those fancy boots anywhere! Cassie is that you?'

'My brother ... ' she gasped.

'It is you! Just hold tight, I'll get my coat. Michael, you may as well come along with me as you're awake.'

Cassie closed her eyes and tried to catch her breath. The pain in her chest was almost unbearable, worse than the stitch she thought it was. She just hoped she'd been quick enough and that the doctor would be in time.

Even above the wind, she could hear the thunderous crashing of the waves. Her wet hair dripped into her eyes and she became vaguely aware of the housekeeper advancing on her with a towel.

'You're bleeding, are you all right?'

She looked up into Michael's face

and his features swam in hazy ripples before her eyes. She tried to say something, but was too dizzy to speak. She felt like crying, but didn't know why.

'It's all right, Mrs Percival,' Michael said, taking the towel from the house-keeper. 'You get back to bed.'

'Poor Cassie,' she said. 'Poor girl. If there's anything I can do . . . anything at all.'

Gently Michael towelled Cassie's hair, then wrapped the towel around her head like a turban.

'You should have been wearing a hat,' he said softly.

'Ready, Michael?' Doctor Morgan appeared, his familiar black bag clasped in his hand.

'The girl's hurt,' Michael said.

'Don't worry about Cassie,' Doctor Morgan said abruptly. 'She's tougher than she looks. Bring her along, we'll use my car.'

'All right, Cassie?' Michael helped Cassie to her feet. Her knees felt strange, without substance. 'Lean on me.'

'Hurry, Michael,' Doctor Morgan snapped.

'You get the car started, Uncle, I'll be along in a moment.'

Michael refused to be hurried. He helped Cassie out to the car and by the time they got there, the engine was humming.

'Which of the boys is it, Cassie?' Doctor Morgan said.

'I . . . I don't know,' Cassie said weakly. 'My stepmother just asked me to fetch you.'

The drive took less than five minutes and even though the doctor drove slowly, the gusting wind blew the vehicle to the side of the road several times, so that the tyres caught in the river of rain that ran along the gutter.

Instead of feeling better when they reached home, Cassie felt worse. Doctor Morgan steamed on ahead while she and Michael took it more slowly.

It was only as they entered the hall that the fug in her mind began to clear and for the first time, she stopped to wonder why her father hadn't gone for the doctor. Had she only imagined that she heard him coming home?

Realisation hit her at the exact moment Ivy appeared on the stairs, her face white, her hair still loose about her shoulders.

Doctor Morgan was unwinding his scarf from his neck and handing it to Mary.

'It's James,' Ivy cried. 'Oh, Philip, thank goodness you're here!'

'Let's have some light on the subject, shall we?' the doctor said, snapping on the hall light before Ivy could stop him. By now, her concern for her husband overrode her fear of electricity and she didn't protest.

'I won't work in the dark! Those days are behind us, thank heaven.'

Two little white faces appeared looking through the landing rails and Mary rushed up the stairs, shooing the two little boys back to their bedroom.

The hall began to spin around Cassie and suddenly her legs gave way beneath her. If it hadn't been for Michael standing close by, she would have fallen to the floor, but he lifted her effortlessly in his arms.

'Good lord,' Doctor Morgan muttered. 'You'd better see to her, Michael. It's probably shock.'

Mary was on her way back downstairs again and almost passed out herself at the sight of Cassie lying limp in the young doctor's arms.

'Give me a hand, Mary,' Michael said. 'Open the door.'

She ran ahead and opened the drawing room door and Michael carried Cassie into the room and laid her carefully on the couch.

'She's soaked through,' Mary cried. 'And she's bleeding. Look at her leg . . . and her poor face.'

'I think that's the least of her problems, Mary,' Michael said calmly. 'Can you get me some hot water in a bowl, quick as you can?'

Mary dashed off and Michael began to ease the black lace-up boots off Cassie's feet. She opened her eyes and blinked.

'What are you doing?' she mumbled.

'It's all right, Cassie. You're home now. How did you cut your leg, do you remember?'

'My leg?' Her voice was feeble. 'Oh, I remember a slate falling from the roof . . . it may have hit me.'

'It looks like it. You've cut your face, too, and there's dirt in it. Did you fall over?'

He held her chin in his hand, his touch firm, but gentle and looked intently at her face. He smiled and at once, his rather serious expression was vanquished, then his face began to blur and fade.

Cassie was only distantly aware of him bathing her cuts while Mary fussed in the background with towels. She felt so ill. Shivers ran through her whole body and her teeth began to chatter noisily.

'Is it a chill?' Mary said nervously.

'I'm afraid it's more serious than that, Mary. Pass my bag would you?'

*   *   *

Doctor Morgan did his best to calm Ivy Grant, but she was distraught and had been since he told her that James' condition required immediate surgery.

She was a sweet enough woman, but inclined to be hot tempered when what her husband really needed was a firm hand. Prudence had known just how to handle him. She had been just as sweet as Ivy, but with a will of iron. A will, he reflected wrily, that her daughter seemed to have inherited.

'I'll go downstairs and get Michael, then we'll get James into my car and I'll take him directly to the infirmary.'

'Can't you treat him here?' Ivy pleaded. 'He's only drunk . . . '

'It has nothing to do with drink, Ivy,' the doctor said sternly. 'Just stay with him for a moment.'

He hurried downstairs and found Michael standing in the drawing room looking at the reading on his clinical thermometer.

'Michael, I have to drive Captain Grant to the hospital, but I'll need your assistance to get him out to the car. What's the trouble here?'

He took in at once the girl lying on the couch, looking far worse than she had earlier.

'See for yourself,' Michael passed the thermometer across.

'One hundred and three!' For a moment he doubted his diagnosis on the man upstairs. Perhaps he'd been wrong to assume . . . But no, Cassie's symptoms were quite different to those of her father.

'She has severe chest pains and a chill,' Michael said.

Philip Morgan examined Cassie quickly. He knew what Michael suspected and he was quick to confirm the diagnosis.

'Pneumonia,' he said, straightening up. 'Help me get her father into the car, then you can get Mary to help you put her to bed.'

'What's wrong with the Captain?' Michael asked as he hurried upstairs beside the doctor.

'Appendicitis. Severe. It's been a trouble to him off and on for years.'

The man lying in the bed was clearly in agony and obviously desperately ill. Ivy, sitting at his bedside, clasped his hand in hers and wept while the maid flipped about between upstairs and down like an anxious bird.

Between them, they managed to get James into the car, then before he drove off, Doctor Morgan said, 'Stay here. This household seems about to fall apart and Ivy clearly can't cope with Cassie.'

Michael hurried back inside and went straight upstairs in search of Ivy Grant. He found her in the bedroom, still apparently in a state of shock.

'Mrs Grant,' he said gently, touching her arm. 'I need your help. Cassie is very ill, we have to get her to bed.'

The woman turned reddened eyes towards him.

'I can't,' she said and turned away again.

'Your daughter needs you,' he tried to sound firm. 'I know how worried you must be about James, but you can do some good here.'

'She's not my daughter,' she said flatly.

With a sigh of exasperation, he dashed downstairs where he found the maid near hysterical.

'Calm down, Mary,' he said and to his surprise, she did exactly that. All she needed was someone to tell her what to do.

'I have to put Cassie to bed and keep her warm. She has pneumonia, do you understand?'

Mary was willing, but not very helpful. Her hands shook so much that she was virtually useless. She fetched dry nightclothes and helped the doctor to change Cassie out of her wet things.

'Her mother should be doing this,' he said angrily.

'She's not her mother,' Mary said.

'So she told me.'

'What's happening?' David appeared in the doorway, rubbing his eyes. 'Where's Daddy? Why is Mummy crying? What's wrong with Cassie?'

Behind him, Jack stood with his thumb firmly in his mouth.

'Get those boys back to bed, Mary,' Michael said. 'I'll stay with Cassie now.'

He looked down at the girl lying in the bed. She looked so small and fragile with her rain washed hair fluffed out around her face. There was so little he could do for her. The pneumonia would have to run its course and it was left up to the fates as to whether she survived or not.

She would either die or she would live, it was as simple as that. There was no way of telling which it would be.

Suddenly, she opened her eyes. They were vivid, red-rimmed and seemed unnaturally bright. Although her eyes were open, she did not see. Carefully, he closed them, then dipped a cloth into a bowl of tepid water and wrung it out before laying it across her burning forehead.

'I'll take care of you, Cassie.' He spoke softly. 'You'll get well again.'

He thought of her rampaging about the railway station the other day being chased by that lad. She had seemed so happy then, yet when he called by just this afternoon, a change seemed to have taken place. What had irritated him more than her behaviour, was the attraction he felt towards her.

There was a sudden silence outside. The wind had dropped and Cassie was resting peacefully. This was just a lull in the storm, the eye, it would begin again in a while and perhaps be even worse. In its dying breath, a storm could be far more dangerous in its gusting than at its height.

He took the now hot cloth from her head and dipped it again in the water, wringing it out before replacing it.

Just like the storm, Cassie's condition

would get far worse before it got any better.

* * *

Michael Ryan remained at Cassie's bedside for the next two days. Mary brought him food and drink and took care of the boys, while Ivy Grant locked herself in her room, refusing to see or speak to anyone.

As Michael had feared, Cassie's condition deteriorated. At the end of two days she seemed to be fighting for her every breath as it came in short, sharp gasps. Her face was scarlet, her eyes unnaturally bright and the pupils of her eyes unevenly dilated, and the fever continued to rage within her, unabated.

Sores broke out around her lips and just occasionally she would cough, the spasm causing her tremendous pain.

It was during this second day that Doctor Morgan visited the house and beckoned Michael from Cassie's room.

'I've sent for Ivy's mother, Mrs Manderson,' he said in a whisper. 'Once she's here to take charge, you can get back to the Grange.'

'I don't want to,' Michael said, going on quickly when the older doctor looked shocked. 'This is such a classic case, I want to stay here and study the symptoms.'

'If you're going to make a success of general practice, then you must learn to delegate. There is nothing you can do for Cassie that Mary couldn't do. Come in now and then to monitor her progress by all means, but don't make it your life's work.'

He looked sternly at his godson, the lad he had financed through school, the one he hoped would one day take over his practice since he had no children of his own and thought how could he admonish him for caring? He would have done the same thing himself, once upon a time, but Michael had to learn.

'Besides, you must have seen a

hundred cases like this one and you know as well as I do that you can do nothing to determine which course this illness will take. Unless you have another reason for wanting to stay.'

Michael looked away. Did he have another reason? Was he really so taken with this girl that he was afraid to leave her bedside? If so, then his being here was unethical, wasn't it?

Philip Morgan crept into the room and gazed down at Cassie for a long time and Michael could have sworn he saw his godfather quickly brush away a tear.

'So like her dear mother,' he murmured. 'Such a tragic family . . . '

'Uncle . . . '

'All right,' Doctor Morgan sighed. 'Stay here if you must. I admire your dedication, but I warn you, don't make it a general rule. There aren't enough hours in a day to do this for everyone.'

Michael followed him back out to the landing.

'Thank you, Uncle Philip.'

'Don't thank me.' Doctor Morgan shook his head.

At that moment, a bedroom door along the corridor opened and Ivy stepped out. Michael gasped. She looked haggard. Her hair was tangled and ragged.

'I want to speak to you again before I leave,' Philip Morgan whispered, then turned back to look at Ivy.

'Ivy, my dear,' he hurried over to her. 'I've sent for your mother and she'll be here very soon.'

Michael watched as he led the woman back into her room, hesitated briefly when he heard an agonised howl, then squared his shoulders and returned to the bedside of his patient.

4

Hilda Manderson reminded Michael of a crow. She was dressed entirely in black and had a large hooked nose beneath which her mean mouth was down-turned.

She stood in the doorway looking at the girl in the bed.

'Under the circumstances,' she said coldly, 'it may be better for everyone concerned if she died.'

Then she turned around and walked off. Michael looked at Mary who had been in the process of collecting his dinner tray when Mrs Manderson had appeared. Mary's mouth was open, her eyes wide.

'She's never liked Cassie, that one,' she muttered.

'Did she really say what I think she said?' Michael asked.

Mary nodded. 'She adores the boys,

but she's never liked Cassie. She didn't like the Captain much either . . . ' Her eyes filled with tears and a sob tore at her throat as she fled from the room.

Michael shook his head. This was, indeed, a strange household.

Another four days passed and Cassie's temperature dropped rapidly. Her cough ceased and she began to sweat profusely. The crisis Michael had been praying for, had occurred and Cassie fell into a deep, restful sleep.

All week, Michael had been reading aloud to Cassie from the books that lined the shelves in her bedroom. He was reading aloud from Anne of Green Gables, when he sensed a presence behind him.

Turning, he saw the crow, standing in the doorway.

'Mary tells me that it's over,' she said coldly.

'She's going to get better if that's what you mean,' Michael replied coolly, marking his place with a piece of paper and closing the book.

'Have you told her yet?'

'There'll be time enough when she wakes,' he said. 'Besides, isn't it up to her mother to . . . '

'Ivy is not that girl's mother.' The crow looked offended.

'I know that, but she is all this girl has now.'

Hilda Manderson stuck out her chin and almost smiled.

'I have packed the boys off to stay with my sister in Epping Forest. Ivy needs time on her own to adjust and to get over her loss. Quite what I shall do with this young lady . . . ' she sighed.

'Why do anything with her?' Michael asked. 'Cassie seems quite responsible to me. I'm sure she will be a comfort to her . . . to Mrs Grant.'

Mrs Manderson entered the room and her eyes swept along the endless shelves of books.

'Such a waste of money.' She sniffed.

'Money spent on books can never be wasted,' Michael said.

'I agree. The money was wasted on

her. She's got too much of her mother in her to ever make anything of herself.'

'I believe she's going to be a teacher.'

'Is that so?' Mrs Manderson did smile this time, but the mouth was still turned down. 'Then you have been misinformed, Dr Ryan, quite sadly, misinformed.'

* * *

Cassie's entire body ached and she felt curiously light-headed and weak. She tried to remember what day it was, but couldn't unscramble the confusion in her mind. It all came back to her slowly, piece by agonising piece.

The terrible row at home, her father storming off and coming home much later, the worse for drink.

Snatches of something else flitted through her mind. A storm? Running through the night . . . someone ill. It was difficult to separate the reality from the nightmare.

She opened her eyes and stared up at

64

the ceiling. It was light, the day was still and gradually she became aware of a voice close by, speaking familiar words. Turning her head, she saw Michael Ryan sitting by her bed, an open book on his lap from which he was reading aloud.

Cassie closed her eyes again, remembering the book, 'An Old Fashioned Girl' by Louisa May Alcott.

'She was ill when she wrote it,' she murmured and Michael abruptly stopped reading.

'Cassie . . . ' He put the book down and stood up, placing his hand gently on her forehead.

'Why are you reading to me?' she said and he smiled at her. He had a good smile, she thought, genuine and warm like her father's. She ran her tongue over her dry, cracked lips and asked herself again, what was he doing here?

'How do you feel?' he asked her.

'Confused,' she said. 'That's one of my favourite books. Did you know that? Did my father tell you? Where is everyone — the house seems terribly quiet.'

'Cassie . . . '

She suddenly felt terribly afraid. Those blue eyes that looked as though they might laugh a lot, were intensely sad.

'You've had pneumonia,' he said. 'You've been in bed for eight days.'

Eight days! Cassie was horrified to have lost eight precious days from her life.

Last time she was ill — which had been a very long time ago — her father had sat beside her bed, reading to her. She certainly hadn't been unconscious then and she felt let down now to think he'd left the job to a virtual stranger, however charismatic that stranger might be.

She looked towards the open doorway. Where was everyone?

'My father . . . ' she began and Michael was too slow to hide the anguish in his eyes.

Although she had grown thin during

66

her illness, Cassie was still agile and amazingly strong. Her hand flew out and gripped Michael's arm painfully.

'What's happened to my father?'

'It was his appendix,' Michael said slowly, trying to meet her eyes and failing. 'Uncle Philip rushed him to the hospital, but he was too late. It had already burst and peritonitis had set in. I'm so sorry, Cassie, your father died a week ago.'

Cassie stared at him for a long time. She felt numb. She even pinched herself under the covers. Wake up, she thought desperately, wake up, Cassie, you're having a nightmare.

'I am so very sorry,' Michael said.

She turned away and stared sightlessly ahead. She hated Michael for this!

'Go away,' she whispered. 'Just get out.'

'Cassie, I . . . '

'Leave me alone, Michael. I never want to see you again.'

He stood up, made to say something,

then changed his mind and strode out of the room. He had seen her through the crisis, had delivered the bad news, now he could get back to work.

He paused downstairs long enough to say goodbye to Mary, before hurrying back to the big house.

★ ★ ★

The house felt strange. Without Dad, it just wasn't home anymore and the boys being away made it seem so much worse. Ivy was nervous and twitchy and hardly spoke at all, while her domineering mother took the running of the household upon herself.

Mary kept bursting into tears for no apparent reason and Mrs Manderson's threats of sacking her just made her worse.

Cassie wished she could cry. She hadn't shed a single tear for her father. Having been too ill to attend his funeral, she didn't even have the comfort of having seen him laid to rest.

A week had passed since her rapid recovery and although she was now out of bed, she had been weakened by the illness and her appetite had not returned.

She sat now at the breakfast table, staring at the food on her plate, wondering if it would have made any difference if she'd run faster to fetch the doctor.

Mrs Manderson had taken over her father's place at the head of the table and Ivy sat where she always sat. A shadow of her former self, moving her fork about her plate aimlessly.

'You have to make a decision regarding the girl soon, Ivy,' Mrs Manderson's loud voice rapped out and both Ivy and Cassie visibly jumped.

Ivy glanced nervously across at her stepdaughter.

'Not now, Mother,' she said.

'Why not, now?' Mrs Manderson demanded. 'The sooner it is done, the better for all concerned.'

Cassie was only mildly curious as to

what she was talking about. In a few months, she would be away at college and need never come back here if she didn't want to. She took a deep, shuddering breath. But she would want to. There were the boys . . . and Ivy.

'It is quite clear that things cannot go on as they are.'

Mary, who had been busying herself around the table, dropped the cutlery tray with a clatter spilling its contents all over the floor.

'Clumsy woman,' Mrs Manderson remarked savagely while Mary, mortified, scrabbled on the floor to retrieve the scattered knives and forks.

Silently, Cassie got down from the table and began to help Mary.

'You see,' Mrs Manderson said triumphantly. 'Cassandra clearly knows her place.'

'Mother!' Ivy cried.

Cassie looked up, her eyes meeting Mary's. Mary shook her head and seemed about to burst into tears again. Cassie reached out and squeezed her hand, 'It doesn't matter, Mary.'

Something was afoot about which Cassie knew absolutely nothing.

She resumed her place at the table, her stomach fluttering.

Mrs Manderson waited until Mary had left the room before speaking again.

'As you are aware, your father lost all his money through those . . . those foolish investments . . . '

'Mother, please,' Ivy said.

'A fool and his money are soon parted they say,' she went on, ignoring her daughter. 'And in your father's case, he died leaving debts and as you know, debts must be paid.'

'My father was not a fool,' Cassie said rebelliously, but there was no conviction in her words.

Mrs Manderson's arched black eyebrows shot up and she pressed her miserable lips together.

Ivy, incredibly, giggled.

It wasn't a mirthful sound, more one of desperation.

'Ivy will receive a small pension and she has a little money of her own so she will be able to remain in this house with the boys.'

Cassie looked at her stepmother, who quickly turned her face away. If she was hoping to find an ally there, then she was to be disappointed.

'You want me to get a job,' Cassie said bluntly.

'Oh, Cassie.' Ivy looked up. 'I know we've never got along really well, but please believe me, this has nothing to do with my feelings towards you. If it wasn't necessary . . . '

'Perhaps I can work in the evenings while I'm at college,' Cassie suggested. 'I could probably manage to keep myself and send a little home . . . '

'You don't understand, Cassandra,' Mrs Manderson said. 'You won't be going back to school. I've already spoken to Mrs Bright about the matter. She was disappointed of course, but when I explained . . . '

Cassie's skin prickled all over with

something that felt like fear, but which was manifesting itself as anger. She wanted to be a teacher! Her father had wanted her to be a teacher!

'It's all been sorted out.' Mrs Manderson leaned across the table, her black eyes glittering. 'We've found you a very good position in a very good household.'

'Go into service you mean?' Cassie gasped. 'But Daddy . . . '

'Your father is dead,' Mrs Manderson snapped and Ivy flinched. 'And I'm sure I don't have to remind you that you have no family with the exception of your half-brothers! And as it is due to the actions of your father that this family finds itself in such straits, then it is your responsibility to contribute to the upraising of the boys.'

Cassie, lost for words, turned to look at her stepmother. Tears were streaming down Ivy's face.

'I'm sorry, Cassie,' she wept. 'I am so very sorry.'

'Just as he wished you to attend

college, it was also your father's wish that the boys should go to the Royal Naval College at Dartmouth. Would you deprive him . . . and them, of that?'

Cassie looked away, towards the framed photographs on the bureau in the corner. There was one of her father, in his Captain's uniform, another of him as a boy in the Royal Navy.

Beside them, a picture of her brothers, Jack and David dressed in little sailor suits. Yes, she knew only too well how he longed to see them follow in his footsteps.

He often spoke to her of his hopes and dreams. She thought long and hard during a silence which stretched endlessly. Growing up had come hard and fast and it had been brutally painful.

'Very well,' she said. 'If the boys' future depends on what little I can bring home, then so be it.'

'You won't be living at home, Cassie,' Ivy said softly.

'I see,' she nodded. 'May I leave the table?'

Ivy nodded.

'Thank you,' she said, getting to her feet with as much dignity as she could muster.

She passed Mary in the hall.

Mary touched her arm. 'Are you all right, Cassie?'

She didn't reply, but kept on walking stiffly towards the stairs with Mary watching her every movement.

She finally made it to her room and once there, all the grief of the past week washed over her in one gigantic wave. The numbness had gone and she was left feeling raw and hurt. She realised that she hadn't even asked where she was to be sent, but then, she didn't really care.

The tears that coursed down her face were not for herself, but for her father, for by cutting her education short and sending her into service, Ivy had finally convinced her that he really was dead and that she, Cassie, was very much alone.

5

Two weeks had passed since the storm, but the destruction left in its wake was still all too obvious outside.

Cassie sat by the french windows looking out over a garden strewn with leaves and twigs. A broken pottery urn lay smashed at the bottom of the three steps and a small tree remained where it had fallen across the path. Pieces of shattered roofing slates were scattered everywhere and there was a patch of damp upstairs where rain had seeped in through one of the holes in the roof.

Jack, sitting on her lap, his head resting on her shoulder, looked up at her while David, sitting at her feet, tugged at her skirt.

'Go on,' Jack said and she awoke from her daydream to look into two pairs of eager green eyes.

'You just stopped,' David added.

'What's the matter?'

'Oh, I was just thinking,' she said and started to read aloud again. The boys settled down to listen and even to her own ears, her voice sounded leaden and monotonous. She had yet to tell them that she would be leaving soon and since they had only been back from Epping Forest for two days, it wasn't a prospect she relished.

As if reading her thoughts, David broke in suddenly with, 'I hated staying at Great Aunt Flora's.'

'She smells funny,' Jack agreed, wrinkling his nose. 'And she wouldn't read to us.'

'That's because she doesn't see very well,' Cassie said. 'And she's very old. Anyway, you're home to stay now . . . '

She broke off, a wistful expression coming over her face. Home. This house is no longer my home, she told herself and no-one has told the boys yet and it's really time someone did.

Closing the book, she put it to one side.

'There's something I have to tell you,' she said. 'Both of you. I'm going to be going to work soon.'

'As a teacher?' Jack cried excitedly. 'Will you be my teacher?'

''Course she won't, silly,' David snorted. 'She's got to go to college.'

'No, that's all changed.' Cassie laughed softly. 'I'm going to work in a big house — doing things like Mary does here.'

'But you can't!' Horrified, David scrambled to his feet and stood right in front of Cassie, red in the face, his fists clenched at his sides. 'Dad would have hated it!'

'I know, but it can't be helped,' Cassie said cheerfully.

'Yes it can!' David insisted. 'We could get rid of Mary! You could stay here . . . you've got to stay here, Cass!'

'It's all arranged,' Cassie said. There was no way she could explain that while it was possible for Ivy to afford to keep Mary on, it was impossible for her to retain Cassie as a member of the household. She didn't understand it herself.

'You won't go a long way away, will you?' Jack's lower lip trembled.

'No.' She reassured him with a hug. 'I won't be very far away at all, but I won't be living here anymore.'

'That's not fair!' Jack spouted.

'You can't go, Cass, don't you love us?'

Mrs Manderson chose that moment to walk into the room and stood, in her long black dress quickly assessing the situation. What she saw was two small boys in tears and Cassie sitting dry-eyed in a chair.

'What have you said to these children?' she demanded, crossing the room and gathering the reluctant Jack in her arms.

'Tell Cassie she can't go!' David said, stamping his foot furiously. 'Tell her!'

'How dare you!' Mrs Manderson turned on Cassie. 'You spiteful girl! Using these children to try and get your own way.'

'I did no such thing,' Cassie protested.

'You're devious and cunning,' Mrs Manderson went on acidly. 'Go on, out of here.'

The boys ran to the door, confused and as Cassie got to her feet to follow them, Mrs Manderson barked, 'Not you!' and grabbed her arm so that her fingers dug into her flesh painfully.

'I don't care what you think,' Cassie said, eyes glittering dangerously. 'So long as you're living in my father's house, I don't even want to be here! I'll be glad to go.'

'This is no longer your father's house,' Mrs Manderson said coolly. 'It belongs to my daughter and her children.'

'No,' Cassie breathed vehemently. 'No, this house will never belong to anyone but my parents! It was built for them and my mother furnished it. Ask Ivy! She's never felt at home here, never . . . and she never will.'

'Oh, Cassie!'

Cassie spun round and saw Ivy standing in the doorway, her face white, tears spilling from her red eyes and she would have done anything to take back those words, but it was too late, the damage was done.

'You see.' Mrs Manderson pulled herself to her full height and there was a hideous triumph lighting her hard features. 'I told you she was no good. Now will you believe me?'

'I'm sorry, Ivy . . . I . . . ' Cassie hurried towards her stepmother, but Ivy drew away as though she couldn't bear Cassie to come anywhere near her.

'I'll be glad when you've gone,' Ivy said softly and unhappily. 'I always thought you hated me, now I know . . . '

'Here, will you be taking this?' Mary held up a cardigan against herself. 'I've always liked it.'

'No.' Cassie smiled. 'It's too small for me now, Mary, but . . . you're welcome to have it if you want.'

Grinning, Mary added it to the small

pile of clothes she was accumulating. Cassie had always had lots of clothes and she had outgrown so many. Mary found it hard to believe this tall, willowy girl had once been such an untidy and gangly child. She recalled the many times she had sat in the kitchen with needle and thread, hastily repairing the clothes Cassie so often tore before Ivy got to see them.

Yet, over the past few weeks, she had changed so much. Not only her personality, but her whole appearance had undergone a dramatic change. Her long hair had been cut into a short bob and this made her eyes seem extra large in her thin face. She had changed from a wilful child into a quiet and self-possessed young woman almost overnight.

She watched Cassie, slowly and carefully folding her clothes and placing them neatly into her bag and something inside her seemed to snap.

'I don't think it's right,' Mary suddenly burst out, startling Cassie into stopping what she was doing. 'You going into service! The Captain'd have a fit if he knew what was going on in this house — how that woman's come in and taken everything over!'

'Mrs Manderson has been a great help to Ivy,' Cassie said, knowing her loyalty was probably misplaced, but feeling obliged to say something in the woman's defence anyhow.

'Help!' Mary snorted. 'You call getting you sent off, help?'

'I'm doing it for the boys' sake, Mary,' Cassie said firmly. 'So that they can go to Dartmouth as was my father's wish.'

'And what about his wishes for you?' Mary demanded. 'You're not being sent away because you're draining the finances! Use your loaf, Cassie. Mrs Manderson has poisoned Ivy's mind about you. She's never liked you because you look like your mother and she was more beautiful and kind and clever than her Ivy could ever hope to be.'

'Mary!' Cassie cried. 'You mustn't say such things. Besides, you didn't even know my mother.'

'Why not? It's true. Everyone knows your mother was a perfect angel! Deep down, Mrs Grant's always been a bit resentful of you and now her mother's here making a proper job of it . . . and succeeding.'

Cassie looked away and got on with her folding and packing and Mary saw the shine of tears in the girl's eyes and felt sorry for the things she'd said.

'I'm just saying,' she said gently, touching Cassie's arm. 'It's not right, that's all.'

When Cassie turned, she was crying and Mary pulled her into her arms and hugged her until she stopped sobbing.

'There, there,' she soothed. 'Things'll work out all right, you'll see.'

Cassie smiled and mopped up her tears with the handkerchief Mary gave her. 'What about you, Mary?' she said. 'Will you be all right here?'

'Mercy, you don't want to worry

about me,' Mary chuckled. 'I heard Mrs Manderson say she'd be off home once Mrs Grant can manage without her and I intend to make sure Mrs Grant can manage just fine as soon as possible.'

'Well, you'll know where I am,' Cassie sighed. 'If I'm needed here.'

''Course we will.'

Mary, to her horror, felt her lip start to tremble and she'd promised herself she wouldn't start crying and upset Cassie. But she'd been with the family a long time and she loved Cassie like a sister.

'I'll come back and see you all, often,' Cassie promised. 'Besides, I'm only moving off up the road a little way. We'll still see each other around town.'

Mary smiled a watery smile and nodded.

'It's going to feel strange working for my godfather, though,' Cassie said.

'At least you won't be among strangers,' Mary nodded.

'There's something else I've been wanting to say to you, Mary,' Cassie went on, becoming serious now. 'I've never thanked you properly for looking after me when I was ill. It must have been a terribly difficult time for you.'

Mary sank onto the bed and stared at Cassie in despair.

'You thought that I . . . ' she began. 'Oh, Cassie, I didn't do anything for you.'

'Of course you did, Mary,' Cassie said.

'No . . . no, I'm not being modest. I really didn't do anything. It wasn't me that took care of you.'

'Well someone did,' Cassie said. 'And it certainly wasn't poor Ivy.'

'No, it was Michael Ryan,' Mary said. 'He hardly left your bedside at all. He must have read every one of these books to you.' She turned and indicated the laden shelves.

'He sponged you down when you were in a fever, washed your face morning and night, lifted a cup to your mouth when your lips got dry. Doctor Morgan kept calling in and telling him he didn't have to stay, but he wouldn't leave you.'

Cassie paled, her eyes becoming large and dark with surprise.

'You'd be dead if it wasn't for him,' Mary added.

'I . . . I didn't realise,' Cassie whispered, remembering with regret the way she'd sent Michael away, then, brighter, went on, 'So, it's his fault I'm alive, is it?'

The attempt at jocularity was a mistake and Cassie's words broke on a sob, but she was quick to take control of herself.

'Don't say that, Cassie,' Mary said mournfully. 'You should never be sorry to be alive.'

Cassie closed her bag and hauled it off the bed.

'It's time to go,' she said.

Cassie hesitated on the stairs. Down in the hall below, the boys were waiting to say goodbye. Jack sat on the stairs while David had draped himself over the bannister. They both looked up at her and she was struck by the misery in their dark eyes.

The death of their father, being sent away to Epping Forest and the nightmare of staying with Great Aunt Flora and now finding that their sister was about to leave home, had all taken its toll.

Little white faces looked up beneath mops of dark hair and Cassie felt a sudden surge of love and affection for them. She would miss these boys more than anything.

Behind her, Mary turned and went back to Cassie's bedroom. She had orders to strip the bed and clean the room right out, as if Mrs Manderson wanted every last trace of Cassie wiped from the house.

Quickly, Cassie forced her legs to carry her downstairs where she dropped her bags and embraced her half-brothers. It was a struggle not to cry, but she managed it, despite the tears rolling down the white faces of Jack and David and the strength of their little arms around her neck.

As always, Mrs Manderson appeared, almost as if she had a nose for such occasions and loomed above them, a look of distaste on her face. Cassie refused to let herself feel intimidated and finished saying her goodbyes without being hurried.

'You both know where I am,' she said, her voice steady. 'I'll always be close by if you need me, remember that.'

The drawing room door opened and Ivy stepped into the hall and Cassie got to her feet and looked her stepmother in the eye.

Suddenly, Ivy moved forward and kissed Cassie's cheek. It was a self-conscious gesture, but one she seemed unable to deny herself. Her lips felt hot and Cassie saw that there were tears in her eyes.

At least she was sure there was no malice intended by Ivy in sending her away.

'The same goes for you, Ivy,' she said.

'You know where I am if you need me.'

Ivy nodded, but didn't speak.

Cassie swept up her bags and hurried out of the door as quickly as she could, her feet tapping down the path towards the gate, wanting to distance herself before the tears she had been holding back spilled onto her cheeks.

She had just put her hand on the gate when Jack cried out behind her and she turned to see him running after her. He was clutching his stuffed rabbit in his arms.

'Take Jojo,' he said, holding it out to her. 'Then I'll know you won't forget me.'

'I won't forget you, silly.' She laughed.

'Take him!' Little hands thrust the rabbit at her.

'All right,' she said, putting her bags down again. 'But I want you to have this.'

She reached up to her neck and unclasped the necklace her father had given her on her sixteenth birthday. It was a simple crucifix, but Jack had always loved it. Carefully, she put it around his neck.

'Take good care of it,' she said. 'Dad gave it to me.'

Then she turned abruptly and hurried away, not once looking back until she was well out of sight of the house and could only see the battered trees lining the avenue.

6

Once around the corner, Cassie slowed down. She was in no hurry to begin this new phase of her life, in fact, she dreaded it. For two pins, she'd have turned and run down to the railway station, jumped on the next train to Liverpool Street and had done with it.

But London was a long way away and this small town was home, however badly it had treated her lately. She was so lost in her thoughts, that she didn't realise she had arrived at her destination until she was actually turning into the wide gravel drive that led to the Grange.

It wasn't until she was approaching the front door that she wondered whether she should have used the back entrance. With a sigh, she turned around, but as she did so, the front door flew open and Michael Ryan shot out and dashed down the steps towards her.

'Ah, Cassie! Just the person I need.' He grabbed her bags from her hands, hesitated a moment when he saw the tattered rabbit clutched under her arm, then ran with them into the hall, carefully placing the stuffed toy on top of the pile.

She was half through the door behind him, when he grabbed her by the shoulders, turned her round and took her outside.

'You're just the person I need,' he repeated. 'Martha Pedlar is about to have twins and as Uncle Philip is at the hospital and the midwife has come off her bike and injured her arm . . . I'm going to need some help.'

'But I don't know anything about childbirth,' Cassie protested.

'Then it's time for you to learn.' Michael flashed her a grin as he opened the car door. 'Jump in.'

Cassie did as she was told, but kept glancing nervously at Michael as he drove through the town, down towards the docks. She tried to imagine him sitting beside her bed, day after day, reading to her, washing her face and as a result, her cheeks flamed red with embarrassment.

He turned to look at her briefly, a quick smile crossing his lips.

'You've had your hair cut,' he said. 'It suits you.'

Cassie touched her hair nervously. Her father would never have approved. Her long, shiny, dark tresses had been his pride and joy and now that hair was tamed and quiet.

'Don't you like it?' he added.

'Yes, but . . . '

'The Captain would have liked it, too, I'm, sure,' Michael said. 'He adored you as his little girl, he'd love the young woman you've become.'

Cassie sat quietly, her hands folded together in her lap, mulling over what he'd said. In the end she decided that he was right, her father would have liked her hair like this and for the first time in ages, she began to cheer up.

The Pedlar household was a tiny terraced cottage which opened right onto the street. Several small children played in the street outside and they scattered when they saw the doctor's car approaching.

Cassie followed Michael into the house which seemed to be full of children still in their nightclothes. A neighbour, who had been sitting in with Martha Pedlar greeted them in the hall.

'She's nearly there if you ask me,' the woman said, looking curiously at Cassie. 'Midwife's coming as soon as she can, but I've got to be off. I've my own kids to take care of.'

Michael thanked her then led the way into a tiny back room where Martha Pedlar was pacing the floor around a bed which had been elevated on housebricks. Cassie gasped. She had never seen anyone so big! She remembered Ivy being pregnant with the boys, but she had been quite slim in comparison.

'Hello, Mrs Pedlar,' Michael said. 'Sorry it took so long. How are you feeling?'

'I . . . ' Martha Pedlar began, then her eyes rolled as she was caught in the grip of a powerful contraction. Cassie was terrified. The woman was panting and gasping and gripping the bedstead so that her knuckles gleamed white with the effort.

'Get some water on to boil, Cassie,' Michael said calmly.

'And get some clothes on them kids,' Martha called after her, completely recovered, but a little breathless now the contraction had passed. 'The little 'un's been running around starkers since she got up!'

Cassie was only too glad to get out of the room. The neighbour had already got pots of water on to boil and Cassie enlisted the help of the oldest girl in dressing the younger children. They were all bonny girls with strong limbs and wiry frames. Each one had rosy cheeks and a head of golden curls.

'Where's your dad?' she said.

'At sea,' the oldest girl replied. 'He won't be home for hours!'

'Cassie!' Michael's voice, loud and urgent, summoned her into the little back room. 'Cassie, come here, quickly!'

Although it was the last place on earth she wanted to be, Cassie sprinted through and saw that Martha was now lying on the bed her knees up in the air, a huge, cheerful smile on her red face.

'Don't worry about a thing, love,' she told Cassie upon seeing the fear on the girl's face. 'I'll be no trouble. It's just like shelling peas with me!'

Michael laughed. 'From what I've heard, you're an old hand at having babies.'

'Right I am,' Martha said proudly. 'I've had six and it gets easier every time. Don't say I enjoy carrying them though . . . Aaargh!'

'What's wrong?' Cassie rushed forward.

'Nothing's wrong,' Michael said patiently. 'Martha's in the final stages of labour.

She's getting bearing down pains.'

'Sorry about that,' Martha chortled. 'It helps me push if I can make a row! Don't mind, do you?'

'You go ahead, Martha.' Michael laughed. 'Scream the house down if it makes you feel better.'

'I might just do that, Doc!'

'You put your energy into giving birth to those babies,' a voice behind them instructed. 'Never mind wasting your breath on all that noise.'

Cassie turned and saw that the midwife, Jessie Mayhew, herself a mother of four, had joined them in the tiny room. She was a large woman with a bush of grey curls and plump, strong arms. One of those arms was bandaged from wrist to shoulder.

'I hope you've got your forceps, young man,' she said.

Martha began to groan again, with a little more restraint now that the formidable Nurse Mayhew had arrived.

'Not you,' the midwife said as Michael moved into position to deliver the first twin. 'You're going to need everything about you for the second one. I'll handle the first one . . . and this young lady can be my hands.'

'Me!' Cassie cried. 'But, I . . . '

'Go and wash your hands . . . thoroughly mind, and get back here as quick as you can. Go on then, girl, move yourself.'

Cassie's head was spinning as she did as she was told. The thought of being present at the birth filled her with horror, knowing she had to take part was like a nightmare.

Events, however, caught Cassie up and before she knew what had hit her, she was gently guiding a head into the world. A tiny head with just a smattering of slick dark hair. The whole thing was so wonderful, that she forget to feel worried or sick or any of the other things she had feared.

'Hold on,' Nurse Mayhew said. 'Don't push any more for a moment, Martha. Cassie . . . '

Michael was so close, that his head

touched Cassie's.

'That's the unbilical cord, around the baby's neck,' Nurse Mayhew said. 'Just loosen it . . . '

Cassie, acting under instruction did just that and within seconds, the baby was in her hands, tiny, slippery and screaming its head off.

'It's a boy!' She cried joyously.

But already, the midwife and Michael were concerning themselves with the second child.

'Wrap him up, keep him warm,' the midwife said. 'When this is all over, you can bath both babies and we'll get them weighed.'

This time, Martha's screams were in earnest and Cassie felt for her. The second baby was the wrong way round and was being born feet first. Despite herself, Cassie found she was watching the whole thing with rapt interest. Michael had to use forceps this time and it seemed to go on forever.

Cassie looked at him. He was sweating so much that it was running into his eyes and he was blinking rapidly to clear them. She got a damp cloth and, as unobtrusively as possible, cleaned his face.

'Thanks.' He looked at her and smiled and for a moment, she thought her heart had stopped beating. Through all the unhappiness and misery, something wonderful had happened. And it wasn't just the birth of this baby . . . it was something to do with Michael and growing up and losing herself in the warmth of dark, blue eyes.

Martha was exhausted, nearing the point of giving up. Cassie mopped her brow, held her hand so that Martha nearly crushed the small bones in her fierce, pain-induced grip.

At last, Martha let out a scream which went on and on and on and made Cassie want to clamp her hands over her ears and shut it out. She was sure Martha was dying, that the agony was killing her and just when she thought she couldn't stand any more, the scream stopped and after a moment's stillness, a new sound rent the air. The lusty, throaty howl of the second baby.

'Another boy, Martha, well done,' Michael said.

'After six girls, I reckon my old man'll be made up,' Martha said.

The second baby was smaller and didn't have the good colour of the first, but after an examination, Michael proclaimed both babies fit and healthy.

'What are you going to call them?' Nurse Mayhew said.

'Well, the first one will have to be Albert, after the old man,' Martha said. 'And I think I'd better call the little one Michael.'

She looked at Cassie and smiled. 'In a way, I wish one of them had been a girl, then I could have called her Cassandra. Nice posh name that — unusual.'

Cassie went off to tell the girls that they had two brothers and to fetch hot water for the bath and Michael followed her.

'Congratulations,' he said and she turned and found his face close to her own. He looked almost drunk with happiness and relief.

'I didn't do anything,' she said modestly.

'You were a great help,' he said and to Cassie's horror, she began to cry and Michael held her in his arms, stroking her hair, soothing her.

'I'm sorry,' she said when she'd finished. 'I don't know what came over me. I don't feel unhappy or anything. It's just . . . '

'A very emotional experience, child-birth,' Michael grinned and kissed her affectionately on the forehead. 'I feel like crying myself! But I have to go now. Will you be able to stay for a while? And make your own way home?'

'Of course,' she said. She could still feel his lips on her forehead, as though they'd scorched a mark in her skin.

'Can we see the babies, miss?' One of the little girls was tugging at Cassie's sleeve and she remembered what she was about and smiling, nodded.

When Michael had gone, Cassie bathed both babies under the watchful eye of the midwife. It was a strange experience, having to hold the babies just-so. Albert seemed to enjoy his bath, going all quiet and seeming to watch Cassie with knowing, slate-coloured eyes. Baby Michael protested loud and long until he was quite blue in the face, alarming Cassie until the midwife said, 'Don't look so worried. There's nothing wrong with a boy who can make that much noise.'

Jessie Mayhew watched closely as Cassie folded nappies and placed them carefully on the babies.

'You're a natural,' she said at last. 'I've seen experienced nurses make a worse fist of it than that.'

She was grinning as she slipped Albert's nappy down his legs.

'Don't be afraid to wrap them up tight, Cassie. Babies love to be wrapped up tight and secure. Try again.'

Cassie re-did the nappy and this

time, it stayed on, secure and she beamed with triumph at the smiling midwife.

She watched as Martha fed her babies, another wonderful experience. Ivy had always fed her boys in the privacy of her bedroom and had become quite upset on one occasion when Cassie had slipped in hoping to watch. The other Pedlar children had gathered in the room and were all examining their new brothers closely.

Still filled with wonder, Cassie hurried to answer a frantic knocking at the door. A small, harrassed looking woman stood on the doorstep, a basket over her arm.

'Has it happened yet?' she asked as she bustled into the hall. 'I got here as quick as I could.'

A howl from the back room made the woman smile.

'I'm Martha's mother,' she said. 'If you want to get off to wherever you came from, I'll look after things here.'

Gratefully, Cassie left the woman in

charge and set off on the long walk back to the big house, home.

* * *

Mrs Percival, the housekeeper at the Grange, smiled broadly at Cassie as she came in through the back door. A tall, well-built woman with long pewter coloured hair tied back in a roll, Mrs Percival was actually a spinster in her fifties.

'Hello, Cassie,' she said. 'Michael told me where you were. Two boys I hear! How is Mrs Pedlar?'

'She's just fine,' Cassie said, dropping into a chair. 'A remarkable woman.'

'Indeed she is. And the babies?'

'Just lovely, Mrs Percival.'

'I'll pour you a cup of tea, you look as if you could do with it. And you missed your lunch, didn't you? I've made you some sandwiches.'

Cassie realised with a shock that it was late afternoon already. The day was almost gone, this day that she had been dreading. And it hadn't been half as awful as she'd feared.

Mrs Percival chattered non-stop and Cassie only half listened as she ate the sandwiches. A part of her was wondering what was happening at home, if the boys had settled down, what the house was like without her presence. Another part was with Martha Pedlar and her newborn twins, imagining the joy in the household when her husband got home from sea.

'There,' Mrs Percival said, with a smile of satisfaction. 'I knew you'd be hungry. I shan't offer you anything else in case it spoils your dinner.'

'Thank you,' Cassie said. 'They were delicious. I didn't realise how hungry I was.'

'Finished your tea? If you don't want another cup, I'll show you your room. You'll find it's quite different to your house in the avenue, Cassie.'

Cassie got up and followed Mrs Percival up the back stairs. She wondered what her room would be like and if she was to be relegated to the attic. She imagined a poor little bed with a hard, lumpy mattress and a bare floor and thought longingly of her pretty room in the avenue with its bookshelves and lace curtains.

She hadn't seen Doctor Morgan for ages and wondered how he could betray her like this. He knew very well how much her father would have disapproved of her going into service. It just went to show, she thought grimly, that no-one really cared what happened to her.

Mrs Percival, who was slightly arthritic, stopped at the first landing and paused for a moment or two, then instead of going on up the back stairs, she moved along the first floor landing.

Where the landing opened out, Cassie paused to look down at the big entrance hall below. This really was a grand house. The doctor's family must have been very wealthy.

'Cassie.'

Turning, she hurried to catch up with

Mrs Percival who was opening a door further along.

'We've put you in here,' she said.

Cassie walked into the room and gasped out loud. It was huge and on two levels. Two steps led to a raised area where there was a bureau and book-shelves crammed with books. The curtains at the windows were old but heavy and good quality as was the bed linen.

Mrs Percival laughed at Cassie's confusion.

'This house is just full of beautiful rooms,' she explained. 'They're all furnished and it's a constant source of irritation to Doctor Morgan that they have to stand empty. There's a beautiful nursery at the end of the corridor, full of toys with two rooms leading off that were once a nanny's apartment.

'My room is just along the landing.'

Cassie was hardly listening. She was moving towards one of the big windows that over-looked the sea.

Someone had already brought her

bags up to the room and the tattered stuffed rabbit had been placed in the centre of the bed. Seeing it filled her with homesickness and the knowledge that whatever happened, things would never be the same between her and her brothers again.

They would soon learn not to miss her.

'I'll leave you to sort yourself out,' Mrs Percival said softly in the background. 'I serve dinner at eight, but if you could come down thirty minutes before to help me . . .'

'Yes,' Cassie said distantly, her eyes still on the water. Darkness was drawing in and the rising moon cast a strip of yellow light across the darkening surface of the sea.

Her father's ship, on her way out, caught Cassie's eye. From this room she would be able to see all the comings and goings of the seaboats and fishing vessels. Perhaps the Captain wouldn't have liked the fact that she had abandoned her education, but she had the distinct feeling that he'd whole-heartedly approve of her living here, in this house, in this luxury!

She shivered, wondering what it would be like to serve dinner to Michael Ryan, knowing she longed to see him again, to be on the receiving end of his smile. Sighing, she turned and picked the rabbit up off the bed and hugged it against herself. It smelled faintly of pencils and crumbly biscuits, it reminded her of home.

Of course, Michael Ryan wouldn't look twice at her. For one thing, she was so much younger than him, for another ... well, her position here placed her awkwardly.

Still hugging the rabbit to her, she went back to the window and saw the ship was no more than a distant speck on the horizon, even her lights fading. The ship which could mean nothing to her now that her father no longer captained her.

The ship which would continue to sail in and out of port quite well without Captain James Grant, just as Cassie would continue to live her life without him. As always, thinking of him seemed to swell the loneliness within her, creating a void.

With a movement of determination, she swept the curtains shut, then hurried to unpack her bags.

Downstairs, Michael Ryan joined his godfather in the surgery.

'Good, you're home,' Philip Morgan said. 'Look at this.'

He was bowed over a microscope and Michael dutifully looked, but his mind was elsewhere. Philip Morgan was quick to see this.

'Thinking about leaving us, Michael?' he said.

'I should be,' Michael said. 'I've another ten months to complete at the hospital before I can join you here permanently.'

'I daresay this brief spell in general practice has done you some good,' Philip Morgan said. 'But you'll be wanting to see Katherine again, no doubt.'

Michael shot his godfather a look, his face paling visibly at the mention of her name.

'It's all right.' The older man laughed. 'I know all about Katherine Charles, although I must admit, I would rather have heard about her from you than from an old colleague of mine at the hospital.'

'I should have told you,' Michael said. 'I'm sorry. I've been so busy, it went out of my mind.'

'My dear boy, if you're seriously thinking about marrying the girl, the last thing you should do is put her out of your mind! I just hope you have the sense to wait until you're finally qualified before rushing into marriage.'

Michael smiled.

'I should go back,' he said. 'Thanks for putting up with me. Would it cause any problems if I were to get the train to Liverpool Street tomorrow? Or shall I take the car and drive?'

Philip Morgan patted Michael's shoulder.

'The next few months will pass quickly enough,' he said. 'The car will still be here when you get back! And who knows, when you return, perhaps you will bring a new mistress to the Grange and that old nursery upstairs will see some use after all these years.

7

Cassie made her way downstairs, pausing every few steps to listen to the uncanny silence. Home had always been such a busy, noisy place and the quiet here was almost unnerving.

In the kitchen, Mrs Percival was loading serving dishes into the dumb waiter and she turned to smile at Cassie.

'Ah, there you are,' she said. 'All settled now?'

'Yes, thank you,' Cassie said. 'What can I do?'

'You know where the dining room is, don't you?' Mrs Percival said. 'I've already set the table, but if you could pop up and unload these dishes.'

'Right,' Cassie said, hurrying back up the kitchen stairs. She wondered if she should be wearing an apron or something over her plain navy blue dress.

She reached the dining room and stopped dead in the doorway. The table was set for four, but informally with all four places at one end of the huge table. So, they were expecting company, Cassie thought as she ran her fingertips lightly over the highly polished wood.

She wondered who.

For a second, she lingered there, gazing at the table and remembering times past when she had come here as a guest with her father and Ivy. Then, every chair had been taken and the huge candelabra had flickered in the centre of the table, the light reflected in the crystal glasses.

There had been so much laughter then . . .

Mrs Morgan, Aunt Violet as Cassie knew her, had been alive then. She'd been a lovely woman, plump and soft with pepper-coloured hair and gentle, hazel eyes. She'd never been able to have children of her own and had always been fond of Cassie, making her welcome, taking her down to the kitchen to try out a new batch of cakes or scones that Mrs Percival had just made.

'Oh, just one, Dorothy,' she said when Mrs Percival looked a bit stern and the housekeeper would soften and fetch a plate from the dresser.

'I supposed you'd like some lemonade to go with that,' she'd say and out would come the big earthenware jug. Her eyes misted over just as the dumb waiter squealed and squeaked into position and she was brought back to her senses with a jolt.

Quickly, she opened the double doors and using the cloth Mrs Percival had left folded on top of one of the dishes, she carried the servers to the table. Aware that this was her first task in the house, she went to great pains to make sure the dishes looked exactly right before hurrying back in the direction of the kitchen stairs.

'Where are you off to?' Mrs Percival appeared. She was no longer wearing her apron and looked quite smart in a black dress with a small white lace collar.

'Go and ring the dinner bell, Cassie,' she went on without waiting for a reply. 'It's on the hall table. Be sure to ring it nice and loud now, the last time I looked they had their heads bent over a microscope and seemed quite engrossed in what they were doing. Although what they find so interesting about a few germs is beyond me. They're quite bad enough, without wanting to see them magnified!'

Cassie did as she was told and, picking up the big brass bell, began to ring it vigorously. She'd forgotten how the bell used to warn them that dinner was ready.

'Come along.' Mrs Percival beckoned her into the dining room and Cassie assumed she would be needed to serve the food.

'When are the guests arriving?' she said.

'Guests?' Mrs Percival said, looking shocked. 'Hasn't the doctor spoken to you about your position here yet, Cassie?'

She shook her head.

'You sit beside me. We shan't wait for the men to arrive — I know from past experience they could be some time and we don't stand on ceremony here unless the occasion demands it.'

Cassie sank into a chair. At home, Mary always ate on her own in the kitchen, no matter whether the occasion demanded it or not. It was a practice Cassie had always found distasteful, but one on which Ivy insisted despite protests from her husband and step-daughter.

'Sorry to keep you,' Doctor Morgan said cheerfully when he arrived with Michael a few minutes later. 'I'm glad to see you didn't wait.'

Cassie smiled nervously and caught Michael's eye. His smile was broad and encouraging and she recalled how close to him she had felt at the Pedlar house. They had shared something very special. She wondered, was it possible that she was a little in love with him?

'Have you settled in, Cassie?' Doctor Morgan said as he helped himself to food from the serving dishes. 'Do you like your room?'

'It's lovely,' she said.

'So, you think you may be happy here?' He paused and smiled.

'I'm sure I will,' she replied.

The atmosphere around the table was relaxed and friendly, more like a family gathering than a mixture of masters and servants. Cassie wondered just how much Ivy's views and attitudes had coloured her own thinking. Mrs Manderson, who had been brought up in the Victorian era held some very old-fashioned and rigid notions and she was a strong influence on Ivy.

Once again, she caught Michael's eye. It seemed that every time she looked at him, he was looking right back at her. She felt herself blush because she couldn't help but remember how it had felt when he put his arms around her and the light touch of his lips on her forehead could almost still be felt.

Suddenly, he winked and Cassie was so disconcerted that she looked away.

She was used to boys winking at her — like Henry for instance, but Michael was different, her feelings towards him were different. For the first time in an age, Cassie cleared her plate of food. It was the only way she could occupy herself.

'I have some news for you, Mrs Percival,' Doctor Morgan said. 'Michael will be leaving us tomorrow. He'll be getting the London boat train in the morning.'

'Oh, so soon!' Mrs Percival cried. 'You've hardly been here any time at all. You will be coming back to see us again, won't you?'

Michael was staring at Cassie and she found herself staring back. Why did the thought of him going away make her feel so wretched?

'You never know,' Doctor Morgan chuckled. 'The next time Michael comes to stay, he may bring his fiancée with him.'

'Fiancée?' Mrs Percival shrieked. 'You're a dark horse, Michael. You've never said . . . '

Michael was still looking at Cassie. She hoped the shock she felt didn't show on her face. Of course he'd have a fiancée. He was an attractive man, but the way he was looking at her now, made Cassie feel as though he could see right through her.

'Uncle Philip's jumping the gun a bit,' he said eventually. 'Katherine and I . . . '

The rest of his words jumbled in Cassie's brain. Katherine. What was she like? Did she work at the hospital in London, too? Had she shared many experiences with Michael like the one Cassie had thought so special?

'To make a success of general practice, a doctor needs a handsome and sympathetic wife,' Doctor Morgan stated. 'I should know. My own Violet was one of the best.'

Cassie's head was spinning. She'd been to the cinema with one or two boys, had even let them kiss her on the lips in the back row, but that had just been innocent, childish fun. She'd never felt anything like she was feeling now.

'You're very quiet, Cassie,' Doctor Morgan said. 'Are you sure everything is all right?'

'Yes, thank you,' she said.

'Don't thank me. When I agreed to be your godfather, I promised your parents that if anything ever happened to them, that I'd take care of you. Ivy's mother would have sent you off to the factory for two pins, which is why I had to tell her that a position here for you would be far more suitable.'

'I think you should explain exactly what Cassie's position is,' Mrs Percival said. 'The poor girl seems quite confused.'

'My fault. I am sorry, my dear. What with this outbreak of diptheria taking up all my time . . . but that's by the by.

I should have made the time to come and see you, but quite honestly, I can't abide Ivy's mother and it was all I could do to keep hold of my temper on the one occasion we did meet!'

He frowned as though he'd lost his thread momentarily.

'Ah, I was saying,' he went on, beaming all over his face. 'You will resume your education at once and go on to college, as was your father's wish! Nothing in this world can stop you becoming a teacher, if that's what you want, Cassie.'

Cassie was dumbstruck. Deep down, beneath the surface of her confusion, her mind had been working overtime. She'd already decided what she wanted to do with her life and now she was being told that it was back on course.

'What's wrong, Cassie?'

'I . . . I don't want to be a teacher,' she said, not quite steadily.

'You don't?' Doctor Morgan spluttered, his cheeks going dangerously red.

Mrs Percival and Michael were both

staring at her as though she'd lost her mind and she realised that her statement must have sounded ungrateful.

'Just what do you want, Cassie?' Doctor Morgan asked eventually.

Cassie looked at Michael, then at Mrs Percival and finally at her godfather.

When she replied her voice was steady and she sounded more certain of herself than she had for some time.

She said, 'I want to be a midwife.'

*   *   *

It had been Michael's idea that Cassie should see him off at the station and she wore her best red dress and her Sunday hat, tipped at a cheeky angle. She seemed so much better, Michael thought as he watched her, since she'd decided once and for all what she wanted from life.

'I wish Uncle Philip would let me take my car back to London,' he said. 'He wants to preserve it for when I join the practice, but I keep telling him, it will seize up from lack of use!'

'You can't tell Uncle Philip anything.' Cassie laughed. 'You should know that by now.'

'What ho!' Michael laughed. 'You're creating a lot of interest, Cassie.'

Cassie looked up and just down from them along the platform, Henry was standing there on one leg, rubbing his shoe up and down the back of his leg and inspecting it for shine.

'He's been making eyes at you ever since we got to the station,' Michael whispered. 'I think he must be sweet on you.'

'Nonsense,' Cassie said, poking out her chin. 'Henry's just a friend, that's all.'

'He can't take his eyes off you,' Michael went on. 'I can't say I blame him. You do look particularly gorgeous this morning.'

Cassie's cheeks flamed into colour, but Michael couldn't help teasing her. Besides, it helped to hide the other feeling he was feeling. The one which tasted very much like jealousy and which he was trying very hard to deny.

The boat train was waiting for the arrival of the s.s. *Estania*.

Michael laughed suddenly.

'I can't get over Uncle Philip's face when you said you wanted to be a midwife! Were you serious? Or was it just a reaction to delivering Martha Pedlar's baby?'

'Of course I was serious,' Cassie said angrily. 'Why shouldn't I be? I've always loved children, but . . . to actually help them into the world — ' She broke off, searched for words to describe how she felt. 'I want to educate pregnant women, to make sure they get the very best for themselves and for their babies.'

'You'll have to train at one of the London hospitals, you know that, don't you?' he said.

'You think I can't?'

'On the contrary.' He smiled. 'I see no reason at all why you shouldn't be a perfectly good midwife. In fact, I see no reason at all why you shouldn't go all the way and become a doctor!'

Cassie laughed then and there was a relaxation of her previously tight expression. Her brown eyes sparkled, her teeth shone and for the first time, she looked like the happy urchin Michael had first seen tearing around on the railway station a hundred years ago.

'Why not?' he said.

'All those sick people.' She pulled a face. 'I'm not gracious enough or patient enough for that. I've thought about it a lot, in fact I hardly slept all night for thinking despite that beautiful bed! It's midwifery or nothing.

'You see, Michael, it's the first time I've ever really thought of what I wanted. It was my father who wanted me to be a teacher and because it was what he wanted, I was happy to go along with it. But he's gone now and . . . and I don't feel I'm letting his memory down in any way by not going ahead with his ambitions for me.'

'He'd be very proud of you, Cassie,' Michael said.

'I hope so,' she murmured.

'Anyway, when you're in London perhaps we could get together. I could take you to a show, or . . . '

Cassie's look was enough to stop him mid-sentence. She was looking at him as though he'd suggested something immoral!

'The passengers will be arriving in a minute,' she said, changing the subject quickly. 'You'd better get on so you can choose a good seat.'

'All right, I'll say goodbye now, Cass, then you can get back to the Grange. Tell Uncle you want to learn to drive, too!' He teased, laughing. 'That will really make him splutter.'

They were both laughing, but it suddenly stopped. Michael put his arms around Cassie and drew her close, overwhelmed by feelings he had been trying to hide. As he held her in his arms, a small voice inside him kept saying, You're infatuated, besotted. Once you get back to Katherine, everything will fall into place and you'll forget this mischievous imp.

She raised her face to his, her lips parted expectantly, her eyes half closed. Michael had seen many sides to her in a very short time, the child, the sick girl ... He had seen her happy, sad, proud, but he had never seen her like this.

His common-sense screamed at him to make his kiss brief and brotherly, but as he bent his head, his lips found hers and all his senses spiralled out of control.

At first Cassie responded, then suddenly she was struggling and for a moment, his grip on her tightened, then he released her and she backed away, staring at him with something that looked horribly like terror in her eyes.

She was backing away, never taking her eyes off him, like a cornered animal.

'Cassie . . . I'm sorry . . . ' He took a step towards her and she cried out, turned and ran from the station just as the passengers from the *Estania* began to stream on to the platform.

8

Home, in London, was a two-roomed apartment shared with a trainee nurse called Jean Philpot. Cassie settled down quickly, enjoying the company of others of a like mind and especially enjoying the job of learning her chosen skills.

Uncle Philip had been pleased to arrange everything for her and during the weeks she had spent with him after Michael's departure, she had learned a great deal. Jessie Mayhew, the local midwife, had taken Cassie under her wing, vowing to hang on until she was qualified and could take over before hanging up her forceps!

And Cassie had remained at the Grange until after Christmas — that Christmas being the first spent away from her brothers. It was very different to the Christmases she was used to, but Uncle Philip and Mrs Percival made it a very pleasant experience.

All was going well in London. It was fabulous to be in the City in the spring and the parks were particularly pretty.

It was during a walk in Hyde Park that she met George Flowers. He was crouching down, tossing crumbs to the pigeons and sparrows and she stopped to watch, being caught by surprise when he looked up at her and smiled.

'George Flowers,' he introduced himself. 'Currently engaged studying the law at Gray's Inn.'

'Cassandra Grant.' She laughed. 'Currently walking through Hyde Park, but otherwise training in the art of midwifery!'

'Good grief!' He got to his feet and brushed his trousers down. 'I thought it was only old dears who went in for that sort of thing.'

She felt instantly attracted to him and knew at once why. He looked so very much like her father with his sandy hair and ice-blue eyes. Perhaps if it hadn't been for that she would have walked on and forgotten about him. He was, after all, a little gauche and his cheeks did tend to flare into colour at the slightest thing.

'I say, you wouldn't consider coming to see a motion picture with me, would you?' he asked, going even redder, then discounting himself almost straight away by adding, 'Shouldn't have asked. You're bound to be busy.'

Cassie felt sorry for him.

'I'd love to,' she said.

When she told Jean about her date, the other girl was more excited than Cassie at the prospect.

'What will you wear? Will you put on some make-up? Colour your cheeks with rouge?'

Cassie had to meet him outside the cinema and when she got there, he was already waiting, a corsage clutched in his hand which shook as he tried to pin it to her coat.

He was very sweet, good company, but all the time she was with him, Cassie could think only of Michael.

Angrily, she told herself that he wouldn't give her a second thought when he was with Katherine, so why should she waste her life fretting over him?

Because she was in love with him, that's why. She knew it now. She had suspected as much before he kissed her on the station, but after that, it had become a certainty. How could she ever fall in love with anyone while she felt like this about Michael? Was she doomed to spend the rest of her life pining for him?

George, who was suffering from an extreme lack of confidence asked Cassie out again by apologising for being such rotten company.

'But you're not,' she told him truthfully. 'You're very pleasant to be with, George.'

'Then you'll come?'

What could she say.

Matters were made worse a few days later when Cassie was getting ready for a date with George. Jean looked out of the window and said, 'Who's this?'

Cassie joined her and looked down at the street below. The man hurrying across the road, his open overcoat flapping behind him, a hat set jauntily on his head, a large bunch of flowers held in his hand could only be . . .

'Michael,' she whispered. 'What's he doing here?'

'You know him?' Jean looked shocked. 'Goodness, and I thought you were such a quiet little thing!'

'I can't see him, Jean,' Cassie said desperately. 'Tell him I'm not here . . . tell him anything, but I don't want to see him.'

Jean opened the door when Michael knocked and Cassie pressed herself up against the wall behind it, holding her breath, her heart going into double speed when she heard his voice.

'Is Cassie here?'

'I'm sorry, you've just missed her.'

'Are you expecting her back soon?'

'I'm afraid not,' Jean said apologetically. 'She's off for the evening.'

'My name's Michael Ryan, would you tell her I called and . . . and give her these.'

'Certainly,' Jean said. 'Anything else you want me to say?'

'Tell her . . . Just tell her I called, thank you. And . . . and I'll call again some other time.'

'You've got to be out of your mind!' Jean said, when she'd shut the door. She handed the flowers to Cassie.

'Why didn't you want to see him?'

'I just didn't.' Cassie shrugged, taking the flowers. 'And if he calls again, would you please tell him I'm out?'

'Are you in love with George, is that it?'

'No,' Cassie said softly. 'I'm not in love with George.'

★ ★ ★

Michael walked out into the street, his heart heavy. Cassie had been there. He'd seen her reflection in a mirror. She was hiding behind the door. He'd

137

felt so happy that he was going to see her again and now he just felt wretched and miserable.

Gloomily and with nowhere else to go, he went into a cafe across the street. It was near deserted in there and Michael was glad of the solitude.

He hardly noticed the gauche young man walking down the opposite side of the street. He had a rather long neck, sandy coloured hair and he was clasping a small box in his hands. Michael barely even gave it a second thought when that young man went to the building further down the street, but when, a few minutes later, the young man walked back, this time with Cassie on his arm, Michael had to take notice.

So that's why Cassie was hiding, he thought. She has a boyfriend.

He paid for his tea and scones and left the cafe, hunching his shoulders against the sudden spring chill. He wouldn't try to see Cassie again.

It was over a year after Cassie left the Grange, that she found herself getting off the London train and stepping onto the familiar platform. She hesitated for a moment, not noticing the swirling flurries of snow which surrounded her, swamped by a multitude of memories.

How things had changed since she left.

She remembered when this was a busy, bustling place, when cargo trains continually chattered from the other platform, when working men always had somewhere to go.

Now the shipbuilding yard was silent, her father's ship and the *Estania* were laid up in the river, their crews struggling to keep their families on the wages paid for a three day week.

She hadn't come back even for Christmas, choosing to stay in London with Jean. Jean, who by some strange turn in events had actually fallen hook, line and sinker for George. Cassie hadn't minded. She'd been glad that

George had found someone who could really give themselves to him.

She had written to Uncle Philip, explaining and reassuring him that as soon as her midwifery course was finished, she'd be with him all the time.

Tears stung her eyes. The midwifery course had finished now and Cassie was in possession of a certificate presented by the Central Midwives' Board.

The platform, despite having been salted, was slippery underfoot and Cassie moved cautiously towards the station exit.

'Hello, Henry,' she said, relieved to see a familiar, friendly face.

'Hello, Cassie.' He grinned. How he'd changed in a year. Marriage, a baby and responsibilities had given maturity to his features, a wife who also happened to be a good cook had added pounds to his weight.

'Are you back to stay?' he asked, looking pointedly at her luggage piled on a trolley and being pushed by a junior porter.

'Yes,' she said softly.

She had grown more beautiful. Although she had remained slim, her features had lost their gaunt look, but she had retained the haunted expression in her eyes which made her seem almost mysterious. She was self-assured, confident and so far, very happy and content with her chosen career.

'Cass!'

She looked up and saw Michael hurrying towards her. Her heart skipped a beat at the sight of him. After all this time, he could still stir the same feelings within her. She had lived for a long time on the memory of that last kiss. If it hadn't been for Katherine, his intended, she would never have run away from him. But she knew better than to let herself get hurt.

Perhaps Michael being here had been the real reason she hadn't come home for Christmas, for he had returned to join the practice last autumn.

She had to face him now. He wore a

black armband, seeing that brought it all home to her . . . the reason why she had finally come back. He went to kiss her and she turned her cheek so that his lips brushed her face.

'Hello, Michael,' she said. 'Thank you for coming to meet me.'

'I'm glad you're here,' he said. 'Mrs Percival is beside herself, perhaps you'll be able to help. The funeral is tomorrow.' He glanced up at the deep grey sky. 'I hope it doesn't snow anymore, it's going to be bleak enough as it is.'

She stared at Michael. He was talking too fast, pouring out words as if by doing that, he could keep his grief at bay.

'Did Uncle Philip know he was dying?' she said.

Michael looked away for a moment as if composing himself.

'He knew he had cancer,' he said finally. 'He didn't tell anyone, but that was just typical of him.' He turned and addressed the young porter. 'My car's just outside, would you put Miss Grant's luggage in the boot, please?'

'Were you with him?'

'Yes.' Michael's eyes dropped and Cassie realised the memory was still painful. 'The miraculous thing was, his death was virtually painless and very quick.'

'And you'll be taking over the practice now?'

'Yes.' He straightened his shoulders. 'Jessie will be glad you're here, too,' he added. 'She had another fall, on the ice this time and she's injured her ankle. Reckons she's getting too old for all this rushing around.' He laughed then. 'I know times are hard, but we seem to be having a population boom here. Martha Pedlar's had another boy, by the way, and practically every other woman you see is pregnant!'

Cassie slipped as they made their way towards the car and Michael grabbed her just in time to stop her going over.

'Mind how you go,' he said. Their eyes met for the first time and she looked away quickly.

He opened the passenger door for her and she slid gratefully into the seat. All the way to the Grange, she stared out of the window at the town which was at once familiar and unfamiliar. It was too quiet. Despite the cold, groups of men stood around on street corners smoking cigarettes and stamping their feet to keep warm. Worst of all, some of the shops had closed and were boarded up.

The docks and the shipyard were unnaturally quiet. It was like coming home to a ghost town.

'You said that Mrs Percival has taken Uncle Philip's death badly,' Cassie murmured. 'Did she know?'

'Whether he told her or not, she knew,' Michael confirmed. 'She knew him better than anyone. In fact . . . ' he hesitated for a moment. 'On the night Uncle Philip died, I'm afraid I gave her a little too much brandy and she got a bit tipsy. She kept going on about his terrible secret and how it had haunted him all his life.

'Did you think he looked like a haunted man? I certainly didn't. Anyway, she reckoned he died with a clear conscience whatever that means. I think if Uncle Philip had any dark secrets, then they should remain just that.'

'Poor Mrs Percival,' Cassie said.

'Cassie.' Michael drew the car into the side of the road just before they reached the Grange. 'There's something I have to say to you.'

'Yes?' Cassie's heart began to race.

'That day you saw me off at the station . . . ' he began. 'When I kissed you . . . '

She couldn't bring herself to look at him.

'I just wanted to apologise. It was a terrible mistake and I'm very sorry if I hurt or offended you. Am I forgiven?'

'Of course you are.' She smiled, although his words were the last she wanted to hear. She'd longed for him to say it wasn't a mistake, that he meant it, that he had been thinking of nothing else since he last saw her. But of course, there was Katherine . . .

'I did come to see you in London,' he went on. 'But you were out.'

'You just came the once,' she said.

'I was very busy,' he said. 'I know I said I'd try to get to see you a bit more often, but . . . you know how it is. I had a lot on.'

Cassie nodded. She had suspected as much when he never followed up his first call.

'I expect they were queuing up to take you out,' he went on nervously. 'Was there . . . anyone special?'

'Not really,' she said. The cold was beginning to get to her and she started to shiver.

'Sorry, you're getting cold,' he said and drove on without another word.

★　★　★

Michael had to leave on an urgent call as soon as they reached the Grange and Cassie went to look for Mrs Percival.

They embraced, then Mrs Percival nodded towards the table where she had a pot of tea all ready.

She had aged twenty years. Her hand shook as she poured tea and her eyes were continually filling with tears. Despite this, all she seemed to want to do was talk and Cassie was well prepared to listen.

'It's as if he was holding on until Michael could take over,' she said. 'I watched him getting thinner and thinner and he wouldn't let me tell anyone, though I wanted to.'

She broke off, bit her lip.

'I remember one year when he overheard me telling Mrs Morgan that I'd seen a wonderful hat in Robjohns. The next thing, he'd been out and bought it for me. 'I can't wear this' I said. 'It's meant for someone much younger'. Well, he just took it out of the box and placed it on my head and he said, 'You're not even as old as I am, Dorothy, and I'm just a lad, so wear the hat and hold your head high'.

'Of course, the hat's old now, but I still have it tucked away in the box. Did you know, he had a passion for bread pudding . . . '

Cassie listened as Mrs Percival talked and as she watched, she saw the strain beginning to leave the older woman's face.

'Tell me about London,' Mrs Percival said suddenly. 'Did you have a nice place to live? Did you see any shows?'

Cassie found herself telling Mrs Percival about Jean with whom she had shared a room, about the shops, the parks and the unique atmosphere that was the capital city.

Mrs Percival seemed to be listening, but just as suddenly as before, she changed tack again.

'It's going to feel very different now there's to be a new mistress at the Grange.'

Cassie's stomach turned over. Of course, Katherine would be mistress here now.

'I'm sure Katherine will manage very

well,' Cassie said.

Mrs Percival laughed.

'Oh no,' she said. 'Michael's fiancée will not be mistress of the Grange. You will.'

'Me?' Cassie laughed now, with disbelief and wonder. 'How can that be. Surely as Michael's wife . . . '

'You obviously don't know,' Mrs Percival interrupted. 'I expect Michael was waiting for the right moment, but . . . I see no harm in you being told. You have inherited the Grange with Michael as Trustee until you are twenty-five. You are the new mistress of the Grange.'

★   ★   ★

Cassie hesitated with her hand resting on the gate. The house looked just the same, yet different somehow. Her heart was hammering against her ribs and she wanted to turn and run, afraid to go in and face rejection. She wouldn't blame the boys if they did reject her. After all, she hadn't stayed close as she had

149

promised, but had gone off to London to pursue her own career.

With a determined movement, she pushed the gate open and hurried up the path and knocked on the door.

Mary answered, stared in disbelief for a moment, then promptly burst into tears and flung her arms around Cassie.

'Mrs Grant said she thought you'd be back for the doctor's funeral,' Mary said when she'd finally got herself under control. 'Will you be staying?'

'Yes. I'm a qualified midwife now, Mary, and I'll be taking over from Jessie.'

Mary hurried off to announce her, then returned and told her to go through to the drawing-room.

As she had feared, the boys were restrained, shy, and rather than fling themselves into her arms, they formally shook hands.

'Thank you for the gifts you sent at Christmas,' Ivy said. 'They were very generous.'

Cassie sat down and they carried on

a polite, stilted conversation. She no longer belonged here and probably wouldn't call again. Instead of enjoying her visit, Cassie found herself looking at the clock on the mantelpiece again and again, wondering when it would be polite to withdraw.

'Cassie, I want you to know that I knew Philip would look after you,' Ivy burst out suddenly. 'My mother had no idea how fond he was of you. I'd hate you to think I let you go thinking you were going into service. I wouldn't have done that to you.'

'I realised that, Ivy,' Cassie said.

Another long silence followed and Cassie decided she really should go rather than prolong the agony. Just as she was about to take her leave, Mary came in to announce the arrival of Mr Taylor.

Ivy blushed quite deeply as the man entered the room. He was much older than Ivy with white hair and the boys ran to greet him as though he were their own father.

'Cassie, you should meet Charles Taylor,' Ivy said uncomfortably. 'Mr Taylor and I are going to be married.'

'And live here?' Cassie said before she could stop herself. 'In my father's house?'

The boys were still clamouring around him and he produced a triangular bag of sweets for each of them, then ruffled their hair before they scampered off.

What she saw was a touching family scene. Charles Taylor kissed Ivy on the cheek and grinned at Cassie.

'I'm sorry,' she apologised. 'I spoke out of turn. It's just I didn't expect . . . '

She didn't expect such disloyalty — particularly from her brothers. Had they forgotten their father? Shouldn't she be pleased that this man was obviously willing to accept them as his sons when he married Ivy? Conflicting emotions assaulted her from all sides and she got to her feet.

'I must go,' she said quickly, wanting to get out of the house before she suffocated on her own anger.

'Surely you'll stay and have some tea with us,' Ivy said.

'It's very kind of you, but no, thank you. Perhaps another time. I'm expected back at the Grange.'

'If you're sure,' Ivy seemed relieved. 'Another time then.'

⋆   ⋆   ⋆

Cassie picked her way carefully along icy paths. Snow was still falling in flurries, but there had been nothing heavy as yet. Her breath frosted on the air and the cold caught at the back of her throat. The more she thought about it, the more she realised that she should be happy for Ivy and the boys.

She wasn't conscious of not taking the road which led to the Grange and only became aware of her surroundings when she reached the lych-gate. The church roof was covered with a white mantle of frost and in the distance, she could see the grave-diggers sweating despite the cold as they forced their shovels into the rock-hard ground.

They would break the back of it today, finish it off tomorrow and then Philip Morgan could be laid to rest beside his wife, Violet, in the family plot.

She turned her back to them and found her way to her mother's grave and was surprised to find it still well tended and cared for. Someone had recently filled the vase with evergreen leaves. Her father had always tended the grave, but obviously this wasn't his work.

The scene was different at her father's grave. It was uncared for and Cassie doubted that Ivy ever came with flowers. Last year's weeds had encroached on to the grave and ivy from the wall had spread to the stone.

Furiously, Cassie tore off her gloves and threw them aside, then began to tear at the weeds and the ivy with her bare hands, her efforts becoming more and more frantic until at last she was crying.

See your Angel's tears, she thought. See what you did when you died! She felt angry with him, after all this time, more than a year, for dying and changing everything.

Then she felt guilty for feeling angry and her body shook with sobs of remorse and sorrow.

'I thought I'd find you here.'

She spun round and looked up and there was Michael. He reached down, took her red and bleeding hands within his and pulled her to her feet, then he folded his arms around her and she leaned against him, drawing immeasurable comfort from his warmth.

'That's right,' he murmured, stroking her back. 'Cry. Let it go, Cass, let it go.'

And as she turned her tear-soaked face up to his, he kissed her, a kiss every bit as sweet as that one so very long ago. When their lips parted, he held her face in his hands and gazed down at her lovingly, but it was more than Cassie could bear and she wrenched herself away and began to run at a pelt through the churchyard.

'Why won't you leave me alone, Michael?' she called back over her shoulder.

And Michael, bewildered, just stood there watching her go. When she'd gone, he stooped and picked up her gloves, then made his way slowly after her.

9

The funeral was very well attended, despite the atrocious weather and Cassie managed to keep a tight rein on her grief throughout. Besides, she'd cried all the tears she had to cry yesterday. Her face was pale, serene and her eyes even darker than usual.

Beside her, Michael stood supporting poor Mrs Percival who seemed to be on the verge of total collapse.

Afterwards, when all the guests had left the Grange and it was just the three of them, Mrs Percival appeared to shake off her grief and went about preparing dinner for them all.

Cassie slumped in a chair and kicked off her boots, curling and uncurling her toes in front of the fire that blazed in the hearth.

'You're like a cat,' Michael said, his eyes dancing in the firelight.

'I don't feel much like a cat,' Cassie said. 'I feel cold and tired.'

After Michael had kissed her yesterday in the churchyard, there had been an uneasy truce between them. Things were not the same, nor could they ever be.

'It's been a harrowing couple of days,' Michael said. 'Now it's over and we have to start thinking about the future. I have to talk to you about Uncle Philip's Will, Cassie.'

'I'd rather not,' Cassie said uneasily.

'Things have to be said, Cassie. Mrs Percival told you that Uncle Philip had left the Grange to you?'

'Yes,' Cassie said. 'Although I can't think why Uncle Philip would leave anything to me. He's already done so much.'

'You're not related at all?' Michael said. 'I am distantly. My mother was a cousin of Aunt Violet. That's why he left the practice to me together with a sum of money. But the bulk of it goes to you, Cassie.'

'Don't you mind?' she whispered.

'Why should I mind?' He smiled. 'Until you are twenty-five, I have been appointed as Trustee to take care of you . . . but I shan't interfere in your life. I wouldn't abuse my position as Trustee.'

'I know,' she said softly.

Neither of them had seen Mrs Percival come into the room carrying a tray with fresh tea. Indeed, they didn't notice her until she dropped the tray and it clattered to the ground spilling tea, milk and sugar all over the floor together with shattered china and clattering spoons.

They rushed to her side and led her to a fireside chair.

'He'll never rest if the truth isn't told,' she wept incoherently.

Cassie could smell brandy on her breath.

'I think I overdid it with the comfort again,' Michael said ruefuly while Cassie wrapped a blanket around Mrs Percival's knees.

'Just sit still,' Michael said. 'I'll clear

this mess up and Cassie can make some fresh tea.'

Down in the kitchen, Cassie found an open brandy bottle on the table. Not only had Michael overdone it, but so had Mrs Percival by the looks of things. She put the lid back on and wondered what this dark and terrible secret was.

It certainly looked as if it would have to come out in the open before long, either that or it would drive Mrs Percival to seek refuge in the bottle. And why did it have to surface now?

She searched for another teapot and quickly made more tea which she then carried back to the drawing room. Mrs Percival was asleep and snoring and Michael raised his finger to his lips.

'She's sleeping it off,' he said, smiling. 'But I'm afraid you're going to have to go out. A little lad just knocked at the door to say his mum's having her baby and can you come quick!'

'You're just going to have to drink all that tea yourself then.' Cassie laughed. 'Where is the little boy?'

'He tore off once he'd delivered his message. The woman is called Hannah Roxbridge and she lives at number 4 Prince Edward Street. Can I drive you?'

He helped Cassie into her coat then handed her her bag.

She grinned broadly. 'No thanks, I'll take Uncle Philip's car.'

'You learned to drive!' Michael cried. 'I knew you would. Mind how you go though, Cass, the roads are pretty treacherous.'

All the way to her call, all Cassie could think about was her job. Despite her training, she couldn't help feeling relief when she saw Jessie Mayhew waiting for her. Jessie had to be well into her sixties and her hands were becoming knotted with arthritis. She was getting about with the aid of a stick.

'Damn this snow,' she muttered as she let Cassie into the house. 'I've done my ankle in now — had you heard?'

'Doctor Ryan told me,' Cassie said. 'How is it?'

'Painful and awkward. You try delivering a baby standing on one leg!' she burst out laughing. 'Thank the heavens you've come back at last,' she went on. 'Now I can slide gracefully into old age.'

A bellow from the bedroom had Cassie running up the stairs with Jessie hobbling along at a slower pace behind.

This baby was almost there. Cassie just about had time to take off her coat and wash her hands before she was carefully guiding the baby's head into the world.

'A girl!' she cried within twenty minutes of arriving in the house.

It didn't matter how many babies she delivered and she had delivered a good many now, she never ceased to be astounded by the miracle of birth. The bedroom was freezing cold and she wrapped the baby up quickly in the warmed blankets before handing her to her mother.

'Well done,' Jessie patted Cassie on the back. 'Your technique has improved no end!'

'I can even manage to put a nappy on without it falling right off again.' Cassie said, remembering the last time she'd helped Jessie.

Cassie was still laughing as she went back to her car an hour later.

As she was getting in, she noticed the tattered black bag on the floor in the back. Curious, she got it out and opened it.

It was full of papers, most of them rubbish and Cassie smiled wistfully. Uncle Philip had always been loath to throw anything away. She found some photographs tucked into a pocket and pulled them out.

Most she recognised. There were lots of Violet Morgan, one or two of Michael and one of herself.

It was the one of her mother that made her look twice.

She turned it over. Scribbled on the back in fading ink were the words, 'My darling Pru'.

Cassie felt as though she'd been punched in the stomach. Gathering all the papers and pictures together, she stuffed them back into the bag. When she tossed it onto the floor in the back of the car, she noticed something else, sprigs of evergreens — like those on her mother's grave, scattered on the floor.

My darling Pru!

She began to drive. It was getting dark and the temperature was dropping. She was having great difficulty in keeping the car on course as the wheels slid on the ice.

In her mind, she had conjured up a picture of Uncle Philip. She could see his face, his little moustache, his receeding hair, the mole by his right ear, but most of all, plainer than anything, she could see his dark brown eyes . . .

The more she thought about it, the more upset she got. Everyone had let her down, deceived her, wronged her in one way or another.

My darling Pru . . .

Was it really possible that her mother had been unfaithful to her father? That he wasn't her father at all? Didn't it just go to prove that she couldn't trust anyone. Even her love for Michael was shrouded in deceit for he was already promised to Katherine. She thought again of her father and how her mother had deceived him. And he was such a trusting, gullible man.

That last thought was the most painful of all and the pain was physical in its intensity. Unaware of her actions, Cassie squeezed her foot down on the accelerator, the car hit a patch of ice and went into a violent skid.

As she wrestled with the wheel, the darkening world outside the car flashed by in a blur. She almost had the car under control when it hit the kerb and turned over.

Cassie opened her mouth to scream, but the sound was cut short as her head struck the steering wheel and she slipped into unconsciousness.

★   ★   ★

Michael woke with a start and rubbed at his eyes. The fire had gone down and now glowed with dying red embers and the clock on the mantelpiece ticked away the seconds, loud in the stillness.

The chair in which Mrs Percival had been sitting was empty. The feelings of disorientation were quick to pass and Michael remembered the events of the day. The funeral, coming home, Mrs Percival's upset and finally Cassie rushing off to deliver a baby.

'I've set a tray for Cassie,' Mrs Percival came in, looking far more like herself. 'Just some sandwiches and a flask of coffee. I expect she'll need it.'

'She's sure to be grateful for it.' Michael smiled. 'I'm sorry I dozed off.'

'You're tired,' Mrs Percival said. 'You obviously needed it. It's been a harrowing time for you. Taking care of all the doctor's patients and him, too.'

'I wonder how Cassie is getting on?' Michael said. 'She could be ages yet.'

As Mrs Percival set the tray down on the table where Cassie would be sure to see it, there was a frantic hammering at the door and at the same time, the telephone began to jangle.

Michael was on his feet in an instant and rushing to answer the door. He opened it with his right hand and snatched up the phone with the left and found himself assaulted by a barrage of noise.

Michael barely had time to notice that the snow was falling heavily now and everywhere was covered beneath an ever deepening mantle before Constable Everson was in through the door.

Down the phone, someone was shouting, 'You must hurry . . . '

And in the hall the constable was talking so fast, Michael had great difficulty understanding him.

'Just a minute,' he said, then turning to the phone went on, 'Yes?'

'An accident,' the caller panted. 'Down by the bridge. A car turned right over.'

'I'll be right there,' he said, then put the phone down as he reached for his coat.

'Constable?'

'There's been a motor vehicle involved in an accident down by the bridge,' Constable Everson said.

'Casualties?'

'One as far as we know,' he said, rubbing his cold hands together.

Michael dashed towards the surgery and began putting extra supplies in his bag. The constable followed.

'Have you called an ambulance?'

'Yes, sir,' Constable Everson said. 'But the town's cut off by the blizzard. It's a funny thing, sir, but we were afraid it might have been you in the vehicle.'

'Me?' Michael closed his bag. 'Why would you think that?'

'Well, sir, because it's Doctor Morgan's car, that's why.'

Michael's face drained of colour.

'Cassie . . . ' he whispered. 'My God!'

He ran outside to his car, slipped and slid across the settling snow, almost fell over in his haste.

'You won't drive through this, sir!'

Constable Everson called after him. 'I had to walk up here . . . '

But Michael was already trying to start the car, praying the engine would fire. It did.

'Get in!' Michael yelled, but the Constable shook his head.

'You won't get anywhere in that, sir.'

'I'm not going to argue with you,' Michael said and eased his foot down on the accelerator.

The tyres slid through the soft snow and if a car can be driven by sheer will alone, then that's how Michael's made it down the road.

Acutely aware of the need for caution, especially as Cassie's life may depend entirely upon his skill as a doctor, Michael tried to restrain himself from going too fast for the road conditions.

His eyes burned from the effort of trying to see the road through the driving snow and burned with something else, too. Tears. He loved Cassie and it took this to make him finally admit to his feelings.

She had been so upset when he kissed her goodbye all those months ago, then in London, she had avoided him.

How well he remembered calling at her rooms and while her room mate, Jean, spun him a yarn about her being out, he could see her reflection in a mirror, hiding behind the door. Then he'd watched her set off down the road on the arm of that fair haired lad . . .

Then yesterday, in the churchyard, when he'd made the terrible mistake of giving into his feelings and kissed her again, she had reacted as though his touch was poison.

Perhaps he already knew that he loved her. Why else had he gone straight to London after that first kiss and broken off his relationship with Katherine? Because he knew that if he lived to be a hundred, he'd never meet anyone who moved him the way Cassie did.

If she dies . . .

If she dies, the thought kept rolling around inside his mind.

Down by the bridge, he saw a group of dark figures through the snow. Despite the terrible conditions, many people had turned out to join the rescue effort. Some men from the shipyard, no longer employed, but still skilled, were trying to cut through the twisted metal of the door.

He skidded the car to a halt, jumped out and ran over to them.

'Careful, Doc!' Someone shouted a warning. 'There's a petrol leak. We can't right the car in case the whole lot goes up.'

Snow fell, clinging to Michael's hair and eyelashes. Angrily, he rubbed it away with the back of his hand.

'Can't we get her out?' he shouted.

'She's trapped.' Someone else held tight to his arms. 'We can't even be sure that she's alive.'

'Let me see.' Michael jerked his arm away and laid down on the snow, trying desperately to see inside the car.

'Come away,' one of the shipbuilders urged. 'The car could go up in flames any minute and we'll all be incinerated.'

Michael moved around the car and found the window of the passenger side smashed. He pulled his sleeve down over his fist and pushed the jagged edges of glass out of the way, before slithering through the narrow opening.

She was icy cold, unconscious, but, 'She's alive!' Michael yelled. 'We've got to get her out of there quickly . . . she doesn't have very long.'

Her pulse was weak, her body temperature dropping rapidly.

'We'll have to risk turning the car over,' one of the shipbuilders said. 'I'm asking for volunteers, I won't hold it against any of you that don't want to.'

Every man there stepped forward, including Michael.

'Not you, Doc,' the man who had taken charge said. 'If it goes wrong and she explodes . . . we're going to need you.'

Michael nodded seeing the sense

behind the man's words, but only reluctantly stepped back to a safe distance.

His heart was thundering as he watched. He was thinking of Cassie, trapped inside, dying. He was thinking of all the widows and orphans left behind if the car did explode.

He closed his eyes and began to pray silently.

When he opened them, the car was coming over, the men huddled around it trying to ease its weight gently to the snow. Petrol began to pump from the ruptured tank on to the snow.

'Easy now . . . steady!'

Michael was already forward. Some of the men were kicking snow over the petrol.

'Careful with that door,' the man in charge said as they began trying to open it. The metal was warped and twisted and with every movement unwelcome sparks were being produced. Sparks which could ignite the spilled petrol.

When the door was finally opened, Michael was there as they pulled Cassie's limp body from the wreckage.

Constable Everson arrived just as they were wrapping Cassie in a blanket and carrying her to Michael's car. He was red in the face and gasping.

The car had stuck in the snow and some of the men pushed it free, then Michael drove as fast as he safely could back towards the Grange.

10

Michael sat beside the bed, looking down at Cassie. She appeared to be sleeping so peacefully and her temperature was back to normal, but the sleep was unnatural.

'I've brought you some more tea.' Mrs Percival crept into the room and set a cup down on the dressing table. 'How is she?'

'If only she'd wake up,' Michael said. 'Apart from a few cuts and bruises she seems all right. But I don't know what's going on inside her head.'

'You're tired,' Mrs Percival said. 'Why don't you let me sit with her for a while so you can catch up on your sleep.'

'I feel so useless,' he said. 'There should be something I can do.'

'The doctor always used to say that sleep was nature's way of healing.

Sometimes, when all else had failed, one of his patients would sleep an illness off. He said it was as if the patient's own body was repairing the damage.

'Now take your tea with you and get off to bed. I'll wake you if there's any change.'

Michael smiled up at her. She'd really rallied and got on top of her grief. Wearily, he stood up and stretched.

'If anything happens . . . anything at all.'

'You'll be the first to know,' Mrs Percival reassured him.

He walked out to the landing just as the first grey light of dawn was beginning to filter through the open curtains at the end of the passage. The snow had stopped and a still hush had fallen over the land. In his bedroom, he lay down on top of the covers, too tired to even undress and fell into a deep, exhausted sleep.

Michael returned after two hours and Mrs Percival smiled up at him.

'You're looking much better.'

He went straight to the bed and looked down at Cassie.

'Still sleeping,' Mrs Percival confirmed. 'Shall I get you some breakfast now? You're going to need something inside you before you go out.'

'I won't be going out, Mrs Percival,' Michael said.

'You most certainly will!' she said. 'You will wash, shave, change your clothes and attend your patients! And you will eat a proper breakfast.'

Michael grinned sheepishly.

'Put like that . . . '

He looked at Cassie again, then hurried off.

Dorothy Percival smiled after him. She had thought when Philip died that she would no longer be needed, but the reverse was true. If anything, these two young people needed her more than Philip had.

Looking down at Cassie, she smoothed some of the dark hair back from her face, so white, so smooth and so very much like Philip. So much, that she was surprised Violet had never noticed.

Or perhaps she had, perhaps she knew.

But no. No-one knew the guilty secret that he'd carried with him to the grave. Outwardly, he'd always been such a happy and capable man, but only Dorothy knew of that one thing that haunted him.

And now, it was haunting her.

★   ★   ★

It was late in the afternoon before Michael managed to get back to the Grange. He'd been to see some patients in their homes, a few at the cottage hospital and there had been a number waiting to see him at the free clinic down on the dock.

News of Cassie's accident had spread like wildfire through the town and everyone he saw wanted to know how she was. They all had their opinions of her. Martha Pedlar called her a saint, another woman called her a minx, but everyone wished her a speedy recovery.

With so many people praying for her, he thought, how could she fail to get better?

He was tired. The snow was deep and he'd had to walk everywhere, but while he was attending to his patients, he'd been able to put Cassie out of his mind, but in between times, he thought of little else.

Mrs Percival was in the kitchen, preparing dinner when he let himself in through the kitchen door.

'How . . .' he began as he tugged off his boots.

'She's still sleeping,' she said. 'She doesn't need to be watched over all the time! She's got some colour in her cheeks. Why don't you go up and see her and I'll fix you a snack to keep you going until dinner.'

Michael ran upstairs, but stopped in the doorway of the room. She was still asleep, but her face was indeed flushed and he was overwhelmed with love for her. Her hair had grown a little and fanned out across the pillow to form a silken frame around her face.

If only he dared tell her how he felt and risked rejection all over again. A year in London was a long time though and it was just possible that she had found someone special while she was away.

He sat down by the bed. He wanted to tell her how he felt and sometimes it helped the unconscious if someone spoke to them. It could help draw them from their deep sleep, give them the will to fight their way to the surface and survive.

'When I said I was sorry about kissing you,' he began. 'I meant I was sorry because you seemed so upset by it. I wasn't sorry for myself because as far as I was concerned it was the most wonderful thing that ever happened to me.'

He lifted her hand from the covers and held it in his, then raised it to his lips and kissed it.

'As soon as I got back to London, I went straight to see Katharine, thinking by seeing her I could make myself forget all about you, but I couldn't look at her without thinking of you and wishing . . .

'I tried, but it didn't work out and instead of asking Katherine to marry me, I ended our relationship.

'I think I've been in love with you from the very first moment I saw you, when you ripped my pocket, remember? You annoyed me and fascinated me all at the same time . . . I haven't stopped loving you since.

'I came to see you in London, but you didn't want to see me, then I saw you out with . . . with a fair haired chap. I'm not sorry I kissed you yesterday. I'm glad I did! But if you can't bring yourself to feel the same way for me . . . I'll find someone else to take over the practice and leave. If only you knew how I've ached for you, Cassie. I love you so much.'

He kissed her hand again then looked at her face, nearly jumping out of his skin when he saw her eyes were open and she was looking straight at him.

He wondered how much she'd heard him say and as soon as she spoke, he knew.

'Don't go away, Michael. I love you, too.'

★   ★   ★

Mrs Percival was astounded to see Cassie sitting up in bed with Michael holding her hands.

'I've made some tea,' she said, smiling broadly. 'I brought up an extra cup just in case . . . Oh, Cassie, thank goodness you're awake. You had us so worried.'

Michael cast Mrs Percival a look and she shrugged. So she was worried, she wasn't about to let it show, especially to Michael who was already worried enough for both of them.

Looking at them now, she realised

something else had happened, apart from Cassie waking up. The way they were holding hands, she saw the love shine in both their eyes.

'How did you crash the car?' she said, pouring tea into china cups. 'When the butcher's boy came, he said he'd heard you were driving too fast. The baker's boy said you'd swerved to avoid a dog.'

'I was driving too fast,' Cassie admitted. 'I wasn't thinking what I was doing.'

'Why for heaven's sake?' Michael cried. 'I warned you to be careful.'

'Don't be angry with me,' she lowered her eyes. 'I was upset.'

She looked at the two people she had come to love more than she ever thought possible and wondered if she could ever share this secret with them.

She would be sharing her life with them and knew they would have no secrets.

'I found out Uncle Philip's secret,' she said.

Mrs Percival gasped and sank into a chair.

'I knew you would,' she breathed. 'I was going to tell you . . . I think he would want you to know and maybe . . . maybe find it in your heart to forgive him.'

Michael looked from one to the other, his eyebrows knotting in confusion.

'Would someone please tell me what's going on?' he said.

'Uncle Philip . . . ' Cassie began. 'Uncle Philip was my father.'

'No!' Mrs Percival cried. 'No, Cassie, that's not true! Whatever made you think that?'

'Yes it is,' Cassie said. 'Look at my eyes, they're his eyes. Why else would he want to fund my education? Why else would he leave all this to me? And there was something else . . . my mother's grave had been tended recently, who else had done it, if not him? Her family are all dead — except me.'

She broke off and thought of the man she had always believed to be her father. Did he know? Would he have called her Angel and loved her so much if he knew she wasn't his flesh and blood?

'You're right, they are his eyes,' Mrs Percival said. 'But not because you're his daughter. When he was very young, barely eighteen, he fell in love with a girl called Lilian.

'I was a child at the time, but my parents worked here and I was raised in this house. There wasn't much went on that I didn't know about,' she blushed slightly at the admission.

'When Lilian became pregnant, the Morgans wouldn't entertain the idea of Philip marrying her and throwing away his future. She went away to the country with her mother before the baby began to show — all paid for by the Morgans, of course.'

She shook her head sadly and tears gathered in her eyes.

'Lily died giving birth to the baby and her mother came back with her grandchild and raised it as her own.

That baby was Prudence and she grew up believing her grandmother was her mother. The woman who raised you after your mother's death until she died, Cassie, was your great grandmother, not your grandmother.

'She was a proud woman and wouldn't let Philip anywhere near her granddaughter, but she relented a little when you were born, when Prudence and James wanted him to be your godfather. She couldn't raise any objections without also raising suspicions. Grudgingly, she had to allow it.

'Philip Morgan was your grandfather, Cassie. He never forgave himself for what happened, blamed himself for Lily's death and when Prudence died so young too, he was heartbroken.'

'My grandfather?' Cassie whispered. All she could think of was her father, the dashing captain, the man who had called her Angel, who had adored her. He really was her father and she was flooded with relief. The rest was too far in the past to cause any pain — except to Doctor Morgan.

'He could never tell Prudence that he was her father and how he hid his pain when she died, I shall never know. He loved Violet, of course he did, they were devoted to one another, but if she had ever found out that another woman had given Philip the child she was unable to . . .

'If she'd ever known that you were his granddaughter, it would have made the fact that she was barren so much harder to accept. As it was, he tried not to make much fuss of you, tried to distance himself from you in case his true feelings would show.

'After the Captain died, he saw his chance to at last make amends, that's why he had you come here. Mrs Manderson played right into his hands by wanting to get you out of the way.'

She stood up and straightened her shoulders as though a great weight had been lifted from them.

'I wish he'd told me,' Cassie murmured.

'Well, you know now,' Mrs Percival said and walked stiffly towards the door.

When she'd gone, Michael began to laugh.

'What's so funny?' Cassie said.

'Uncle Philip was a stubborn old devil at times. Now I know where you get it from.'

Cassie didn't laugh. Instead, she said, 'You saw me out with George . . . you knew I'd deliberately avoided seeing you?'

'Yes,' he admitted.

She darted a look at him.

'How?'

'I saw your reflection in the mirror. Why did you hide from me, Cassie? Was it because of George . . . were you in love with him?'

'Not because of George . . . because of Katherine.'

'Katherine?'

'You were practically engaged to be married, remember? And I . . . I was in love with you. I'd already lost both my

188

parents, I couldn't bear to find love again knowing I'd lose it.'

'But you wouldn't.' Michael wrapped his arms around her and held her tight. 'You won't lose me, Cass.'

'I didn't know that then.' She clung to him.

'But you know it now,' he said. 'You know I love you. I want to marry you and be with you forever. Will you marry me, Cass?'

And Cassie, her heart soaring, said, 'Yes.'

The tears that streamed down her face now, were tears of joy and as Michael kissed them away she knew that her father had been right all along, dreams do come true. Hers had.

THE END

We do hope that you have enjoyed reading this large print book.

Did you know that all of our titles are available for purchase?

We publish a wide range of high quality large print books including:
Romances, Mysteries, Classics
General Fiction
Non Fiction and Westerns

Special interest titles available in large print are:
The Little Oxford Dictionary
Music Book, Song Book
Hymn Book, Service Book

Also available from us courtesy of Oxford University Press:
Young Readers' Dictionary
(large print edition)
Young Readers' Thesaurus
(large print edition)

For further information or a free brochure, please contact us at:
Ulverscroft Large Print Books Ltd.,
The Green, Bradgate Road, Anstey,
Leicester, LE7 7FU, England.
Tel: (00 44) **0116 236 4325**
Fax: (00 44) **0116 234 0205**

CELEBRITY VET

Carol Wood

Veterinary nurse Tessa Dance takes on her live-in job in the New Forest with some trepidation. Her new employer is *the* Samuel Wilde, who is accustomed to female adoration, expects 'flexibility' from her — whatever that means — and who clearly anticipates Tessa falling at his feet too. She has to admit he is dangerously attractive, as well as a gifted veterinary surgeon, but trying to understand this complex man is surely playing with fire . . . ?

TIME AFTER TIME

Patricia Keyson

When Kay falls in love with Michael, her boss, she thinks he will always put his business first. Together they discover there are plans to discredit the company, so they set out to expose those responsible. Kay hopes the excellent working relationship they have will overflow into their personal lives, and wishes she knew Michael's feelings for her. In the 1950s it isn't easy to ask. Can she fly in the face of convention?

FOLLOW YOUR DREAM

Jean Robinson

Steph has a successful career, a smart London flat and a good social life. After being badly hurt by the man she loved, she is determined never to let it happen again. When she inherits her Aunt Rose's old cottage in the village where she grew up, she decides to take two weeks to put everything in order and sell up — but then she meets the attractive Rick Jameson . . . Steph has some difficult decisions to make, and things are not necessarily what they seem.

CHAMPAGNE HARVEST

Ann Carroll

Journalist Laura Kane believes that French artist and Champagne grower Philippe Beaulieu is involved in the disappearance of a local teenager. However, the dynamic artist has a passionate hatred of journalists, so she keeps her profession and her journalistic investigation secret. Despite her concerns, love blossoms among the vineyards and she finds the missing teenager. However, when Philippe discovers her true profession he feels betrayed. Their love seems doomed — and to make matters worse, so does the harvest . . .